Hard As Steel

Also from Laura Kaye

Hard As Steel

A Hard Ink/Raven Riders Crossover
By Laura Kaye

1001 Dark Nights

EVIL EYE
CONCEPTS

Hard As Steel
A Hard Ink/Raven Riders Crossover
By Laura Kaye

1001 Dark Nights
Copyright 2015 Laura Kaye
ISBN: 978-1-940887-29-6

Foreword Copyright 2014 M. J. Rose
Published by Evil Eye Concepts, Incorporated

Author Acknowledgments

When Liz Berry called and invited me to participate in the 1001 Dark Nights project, I couldn't have been more thrilled. Getting to work with passionate, creative, amazing people has been one of my favorite things about being a writer, and everything about 1001 Dark Nights delivers that and more. So my first thanks must go to Liz Berry, M.J. Rose, and the other fantastic Dark Nights authors. I'm so glad to get to be a part of this with you *and* to bring my readers more stories from the Hard Ink—and new Raven Riders—worlds.

Next, I must thank my Avon editor Amanda Bergeron for helping me make Hard Ink the amazing experience it's been and for allowing me to contribute a Hard Ink story to 1001 Dark Nights. Everything about working with Amanda has been this author's dream come true. Thanks, Amanda!

My next shoutout goes to the awesome Jillian Stein, an amazing friend, blogger, and social media manager for 1001 Dark Nights. You bring such fun and grace to everything you do for me and so many others, and I really appreciate it.

As always, I'd never finish a book without the encouragement and support of writer friends Lea Nolan, Stephanie Dray, Christi Barth, and Jennifer L. Armentrout. My publicist KP Simmon and agent Kevan Lyon are amazing and indispensable parts of my team, and so often help me make what I do go as smoothly as it can. Thanks, too, to my husband and daughters for always pitching in to help when deadlines loom—you guys are the most supportive family ever and I thank you for that from the bottom of my heart. I appreciate all of you so much!

Finally, I must thank my Heroes for being so awesomely generous with their time and friendship. And, last but not least, I thank the readers for taking my characters into their hearts and allowing them to tell their stories again and again. ~LK

Sign up for the 1001 Dark Nights Newsletter
and be entered to win a Tiffany Key necklace.

There's a contest every month!

Go to www.1001DarkNights.com to subscribe.

As a bonus, all subscribers will receive a free
1001 Dark Nights story
The First Night
by Lexi Blake & M.J. Rose

One Thousand and One Dark Nights

Once upon a time, in the future...

*I was a student fascinated with stories and learning.
I studied philosophy, poetry, history, the occult, and
the art and science of love and magic. I had a vast
library at my father's home and collected thousands
of volumes of fantastic tales.*

*I learned all about ancient races and bygone
times. About myths and legends and dreams of all
people through the millennium. And the more I read
the stronger my imagination grew until I discovered
that I was able to travel into the stories... to actually
become part of them.*

*I wish I could say that I listened to my teacher
and respected my gift, as I ought to have. If I had, I
would not be telling you this tale now.
But I was foolhardy and confused, showing off
with bravery.*

*One afternoon, curious about the myth of the
Arabian Nights, I traveled back to ancient Persia to
see for myself if it was true that every day Shahryar
(Persian: شهریار, "king") married a new virgin, and then
sent yesterday's wife to be beheaded. It was written
and I had read, that by the time he met Scheherazade,
the vizier's daughter, he'd killed one thousand
women.*

*Something went wrong with my efforts. I arrived
in the midst of the story and somehow exchanged
places with Scheherazade — a phenomena that had
never occurred before and that still to this day, I
cannot explain.*

Now I am trapped in that ancient past. I have taken on Scheherazade's life and the only way I can protect myself and stay alive is to do what she did to protect herself and stay alive.

Every night the King calls for me and listens as I spin tales. And when the evening ends and dawn breaks, I stop at a point that leaves him breathless and yearning for more. And so the King spares my life for one more day, so that he might hear the rest of my dark tale.

As soon as I finish a story... I begin a new one... like the one that you, dear reader, have before you now.

Dedication

To the readers, for wanting more Hard Ink! You guys rock hard. So hard.

Chapter 1

Jessica Jakes had been lusting after Ike Young from almost the day she met him, back when she was a newbie piercer at Hard Ink Tattoo and Ike first came looking for a job as an artist. Which meant she should've been thrilled that her thighs had been wrapped around his hips for nearly an hour. Except she wasn't in his bed. She was on the back of his bike. And she was running for her life.

The Harley's roar ripped through the warm May afternoon as they drove country roads, piercing through farmlands and forests. But Jess couldn't begin to appreciate the scenery. Not when her whole world was falling apart. She hugged her arms tighter around Ike's broad chest, and he gave her hand a squeeze like he knew she needed it.

She did.

Ike banked the motorcycle to the right, pulling into a narrow gravel drive sheltered by trees. Jess wasn't entirely sure what to expect. All she knew was that they'd ridden about forty-five minutes west of Baltimore into the rural rolling mountains near where Ike's motorcycle club, the Raven Riders, had their compound. Around a sharp bend, the sparkling green-blue water of a lake further down the mountain came into view. The water quickly disappeared behind another copse of trees before they reached their destination, a tiny white house with a detached garage behind it.

With a columned front porch, dark-red front door, and brown stone chimney and walkway, the place sat sheltered in the shade of several tall, old trees, and had a quaint charm about it. For the first time since she'd learned that she was in danger, Jess smiled. Because hard-ass, no-nonsense biker man Ike Young had a cute little cottage. Who would've thought?

Ike parked, killed the engine, and gave Jess a hand off the bike. She was still wearing a grin when she lifted the helmet from her head and shook out her black hair.

"What's funny?" Ike asked, eyeballing her as he scrubbed his hand over his bald head.

Jess gave Ike a long, appreciative glance—and there was so damn much to see. Besides being *way* over six-feet tall, Ike had a black abstract tribal inked onto the left side of his head, the sharp blades of another abstract tribal reaching out of the collar of his black T-shirt, and tattooed sleeves running down both muscled arms. He was a feast for her eyes. One that her hands and mouth had always longed to join.

"Nothing's funny. Your house is just so…cute." She released her helmet into Ike's big hand.

He frowned as he looked at the house, like he was trying to see it through her eyes. "It's not cute. It's a damn cabin."

Jess smirked. "Okay, well, it's a cute cabin then. Do you even fit inside this place? Because standing next to it, you look even freakishly bigger than usual."

Of course, most everyone looked big compared to Jess. At five foot one inch tall, she made up for in snark what she lacked in height. But that was okay, because she *liked* big. Ike's kinda big.

Ike shook his head and gave her a droll stare, then turned to pull her duffle from a leather saddlebag on the back of the bike. He hiked her bag over his shoulder. "House rules for as long as we're here," he said, staring down at her with those piercing, dark eyes. "One. No leaving without my permission—"

"Where would I even—"

"Two." His eyebrow arched, and he nodded toward the porch, beckoning her to follow. "If anyone comes to the house, stay out of sight."

Jess climbed the two steps and waited while Ike unlocked the door—at three different places. Under any other circumstances, she'd have teased him about being overly cautious, but given her current situation, those locks seemed more reassuring than funny. "Anything else, boss man?" she asked with more bravado than she felt.

"Yeah." He pushed open the door, then stood aside and gestured for her to go first.

She stepped inside, her eyes struggling to adjust to the dimness. The house was warm from being closed up, the air still.

Ike turned on a lamp, casting golden light over the small first floor. The living room consisted of an overstuffed brown couch facing a rustic stone fireplace. A flat-screen television hung over the mantle. A console table sat behind the couch, and not too far from that a two-seater wooden table made up the entirety of the dining room. With its white appliances, cabinets, and Formica countertop, the galley-style kitchen was old school all the way, but clean and neat. Brown paneled walls, wide plank floors, and exposed wooden beams made the house feel like the cabin Ike said it was.

Still cute, though.

A series of clicks brought Jess's gaze to the locks on the door.

You're safe, Jess. You're with Ike, out of the city, away from…whoever the hell broke into your house and tried to grab you. Just breathe.

Right. Breathing. Check.

Except, she couldn't help but feel that she'd brought this whole damn situation on herself. Still, how the hell was she supposed to know that the man she'd picked up at a bar last Friday night had been a bad guy intent on using her to get to her friends? Just thinking of it made her skin crawl and her stomach toss.

"Three," Ike said, apparently not realizing she was having a mini-meltdown in the middle of his living room.

"Three? I might need to write these down," she quipped, hoping her voice sounded lighter than her chest felt. Because Jess *hated* to be scared. She despised feeling helpless and cornered and trapped. Once, she'd fallen apart and let fear get the best of her.

Never again.

Ike was in front of her in an instant, a scowling, unamused wall of muscle and ink. "I'm not fucking around here, Jessica. Take something seriously. For once."

Sweat dampened her neck under her long hair, and anger lanced through Jess's chest until her bones nearly vibrated with it. Anger about the danger Jeremy and Nick Rixey—her employers and friends for the past four years—were in. Anger about the fact that their tattoo shop had been bombed and closed…until God only knew when. Anger that her own house was a shambles, too, after a middle-of-the-night invasion that sent her scurrying like an animal into the crawl space at the back of her bedroom closet.

Anger about being targeted and used and hunted by the very animals that had attempted to hurt her friends.

It was all too damn much.

"Wow, Ike. Thanks for clarifying how serious this situation is. Because I was really confused about what the guys with the guns ransacking my apartment last night meant. So much clearer now." She crossed her tattooed arms over her chest and nailed Ike with a glare. Anger felt *so* much better than fear.

Ike's gaze narrowed, but then his face relaxed and his shoulders dropped. "Fuck. Didn't mean to—"

"Yeah, yeah. Whatever," she said, blinking the sting out of her eyes. No way was she crying in front of Ike. He already treated her like an overprotective big brother as it was. And that was really freaking annoying because it meant her fantasies of climbing him like a tree and having her wily way with him weren't ever coming true. Unrequited lust sucked big hairy donkey balls. "So, what's three?"

"No cell phone, no e-mail, no using credit cards," he said in a gentler tone. "In fact, give me your cell. Just to be sure."

The only reason Jess didn't gripe was because she knew enough about Nick and Jeremy's über-scary mercenary enemies to know they could probably find her easier than she wanted to think about if she didn't stay off the grid. She fished the smartphone from her bra and smacked it into Ike's palm.

His eyebrow arched as his gaze moved from the phone to her breasts and back again.

"What?" she asked, more comfortable with him ogling her boobs than giving her that serious, concerned look he wore a moment ago. "I was afraid it would fall out of my back pocket on the bike."

Ike shook his head and slipped the cell into the pocket of his jeans. Which immediately made Jess jealous of her phone because her hands would burrow the fuck into those jeans if he gave her half a chance.

But alas...

"Anything else, warden?" she asked.

"You're not funny," he said.

"I'm a little funny," she said.

"You're a little pain in my ass," he said.

Jess schooled her expression. Because she wouldn't be surprised if there was more than a little truth behind his words. She and Ike had worked together for years and become friends, but all this was way, *way* above and beyond. When the scumbags who'd broken into her home finally left last night, she'd been too scared to come out of the crawl space behind her closet and hadn't been sure who she should trust. The police were out because Jeremy and Nick had learned that the authorities were in bed with at least some of the bad guys who'd attacked Hard Ink. It was mindboggling to believe that an international drug ring that had injured Nick and killed six of his Special Forces teammates in Afghanistan over a year ago had spilled over into Baltimore. And that Nick's investigation with his surviving SF teammates that had been operating out of the Hard Ink tattoo shop had exploded all over Jess's life. But that's exactly what was happening.

Crouched in the dusty darkness of the crawl space, she'd finally settled on calling Ike. Given his protectiveness of her, his all-around bad-assness, and that he already knew all about the Rixeys' troubles, he'd seemed like the natural choice. But when she'd called, she'd never expected the barely restrained rage that vibrated off Ike as he gently coaxed her from her hiding place, nor the way he tugged her into his arms and just held her once she was out. And she'd certainly never expected him to put his whole life on hold like this. For her. "Yeah, well," she said, forcing the thoughts away. "I'll try harder next time."

Ike's smirk held a hint of amusement for the first time since they'd arrived. "No doubt. So, last rule. No busting my balls."

"I wholly object to that one. I'm already going to die of boredom out here. You have to let me have *some* fun."

Ike got right up in her space, so close that she had to tilt her head way back to look him in the eye. "You think I don't see how you use humor to deflect when you're scared? But I see it, Jess. I see you. So let me be clear. You are *not* gonna die. Not on my watch."

A riot of reaction erupted inside Jess's head. The uncertainty of being laid so bare. The scary satisfaction of being seen when Jess always worked so hard to only reveal what she wanted of herself. The red-hot lust caused by Ike's hard body being pressed so close to hers.

Despite the heat inside the house, Jess nearly shivered at the intensity Ike was throwing off. She became aware of him the way you become aware of the electricity in the air before a summer storm— slowly, insistently, magnetically. Her lips parted as she scrambled for a response, but her nipples were pebbling against his chest, which made her wonder if he'd be able to feel her piercings there.

Ike took a small step backward, but it was enough to break the crazy physical connection pinging between them. Had he felt it too?

"Okay, so, no dying," she said. To her own ears, her voice sounded like a throaty purr. "And, um—" She swallowed hard, trying to gather her wits about her. "—the boredom part?" She peered up at him, hoping against hope that she wasn't the only one as affected by whatever had just passed between them.

Ike's eyes narrowed as if he was on to her game. "Nick and his team know what they're doing. Hopefully this situation will get resolved fast and you won't have to be here that long."

"Right," she said. Jess hoped that, too. She wanted her friends safe and their enemies to be gone. For good. Still, she couldn't help but wonder if Ike was eager for her to be out of here. In all the years she'd known him, she'd never been to his apartment in the city, nor had he ever invited her out to the Ravens' compound for any of their parties or the races they ran at their dirt racetrack. It had always felt like, on some level, Ike held her at a distance. No doubt a guy as hot as Ike had plenty of offers, but Jess didn't think his reserve with her was because he had a girlfriend tucked away somewhere. In all the years she'd known him, she'd never once heard him mention a relationship, nor had he ever brought anyone around. Still, she couldn't help but feel that there was a part of his world he didn't want to share—with her, at least.

And now, here they were for the first time ever, hidden away from the world in a tiny cabin. All alone.

Get a grip, Jess. This isn't some romantic cabin getaway.

Right. Ike wasn't here with her because he wanted to spend time with her, he was here because she'd asked for his help, because he was a good guy, and because he knew she needed protection.

When Nick's team finished its investigation and nailed their enemies, she'd go back to her regular life, and she and Ike would go back to being friendly colleagues with tons of sexual tension and flirty innuendo buzzing between them. It was already embarrassing enough that everyone knew she'd unknowingly slept with one of the bad guys. The last thing she needed while they were stuck together here was to make it clear just how much she wanted and cared about Ike—not just as a friend, or even a friend with benefits—which she'd half-jokingly suggested once in a moment of tipsy weakness. No, she wanted Ike much more than any of that. Despite the fact that she had no chance with him whatsoever.

Which meant Jess needed to put her fantasies about Ike Young aside. Once and for all.

Chapter 2

Ike needed to get the hell out of there before he ended up giving Jess a hands-on demonstration of all the ways he could distract her from the shit storm that had become their lives. Because a distraction of the his-skin-on-her-skin variety was the last thing either of them needed.

No matter how hot Jessica Jakes was—and she was like goddamn molten lava with her tight little body, inked porcelain skin, and smart mouth—she was precisely the kind of woman Ike had vowed never to get twisted up with again. A woman in trouble.

Been there, done that, still had the shrapnel lodged in his heart. Fuck you very much.

Even if Jess did have piercings in places Ike would've given his left ball to see and tongue and suck. Just once. And even if she looked at him with all kinds of invitation in her eyes. Which she was doing. Right now.

But he couldn't just drop her there and run without at least showing her around the place. He wanted her to feel comfortable for however long they had to be there.

"So, here's the dime tour," Ike said. "TV has cable." He pointed to the flat-screen that hung over the fireplace, then crossed the room toward the kitchen. He pointed to cabinets and drawers as he spoke. "Cups. Plates and bowls. Silverware. Basically, just feel free to poke around for whatever you need." One by one, Ike unlocked and lifted the sashes to two windows in the kitchen. "There's no air conditioning here, but the breeze off the mountain usually keeps it comfortable."

"No worries," Jess said, her eyes following him as he moved around the open space of the main floor. "I don't mind the heat. We didn't have air conditioning when I was growing up, so I'm kinda used to it."

Ike nodded. "It'll be nice in here at night, though." Next, he opened the window to the left of the fireplace, and the cross-breeze immediately swept through the cabin. Work as the club's betting officer—the man who took off-site bets on the Ravens' racing events, and collected debts when owed—originally sent him to Baltimore six years ago, and then his job at Hard Ink made it a permanent move. Right from the start, Ike had been into Jess, but he figured the daughter of a cop, even recently deceased as he'd been then, was the last person he wanted to bring into the Ravens' fold. They weren't outlaws, but they weren't angels, either.

He breathed in the clean air coming through the window. Four years later, the city had become home, but Ike always appreciated any chance to get away from the grind and return to the peace and quiet of the mountains, and to his brothers in the club.

He just wished he was there under better circumstances.

Shoving the thought away, he reached into the small room beside the stairs and flicked on the light switch. "Bathroom. There are some towels under the sink."

"And the bedrooms are upstairs?" she asked.

"It's a loft," Ike said, nodding her toward the steps. The second floor had a pitched ceiling that followed the slope of the roof, and one wall that stood only waist-high, making it so that you could look down onto the living room and kitchen table. A queen-sized bed filled most of the brown-paneled space. A small nightstand and a stuffed brown armchair made up the only other furniture in the room.

Jess's gaze took in the small room, and Ike could see the question on her face before she gave voice to it.

"This will be yours," he said. "I'll sleep on the couch. My clothes are in the closet there, but I'll pull some things out so you can have privacy."

Jess's eyes cut from the bed to him. "I'll sleep on the couch."

"Jess—"

"You're way bigger than me. I'll be more comfortable there than you will."

Ike shook his head. The last thing he needed was to be able to see her as she slept. "This is yours for as long as you're here."

"Ike, you're already doing enough for me."

"If I was doing enough, you wouldn't be in trouble in the first place." Ike wanted to bite back the words the second they escaped his mouth. Jess didn't need to know how protective he was of her and how much he really cared. Just the memory of the fear in her voice when she'd called last night and how badly she was shaking when he'd pulled her out of her closet made his blood boil.

Her brow furrowed and she stepped closer. "How were you supposed to know this would happen?"

"Given the situation, I should've planned for the worst-case scenario and had you stay at Hard Ink with everyone else. Jeremy's employees being targeted for information wasn't that big of a leap."

"Ike," Jess said, compassion and affection plain in her voice. She closed the gap between them and rested her hand against his chest. The soft touch shot through him, setting his body on edge and making him want so much more. "None of this was your fault. You can't think that it was."

He wasn't going to debate it with her. Ike wasn't a boy looking to duck his responsibilities, he was a thirty-five-year-old man who fully owned it when he'd fucked up. Because, Jesus Christ, when he fucked up, he did it spectacularly. What happened to Lana proved that. And the same thing had almost happened to Jess. What would Jess think if she ever learned Lana had died on his watch? How safe would she feel right now if she knew how badly he'd let another woman down?

Sonofabitch.

Jessica's hand gripped his shirt, and she softly beat her fist against his chest. "Ike, tell me you know I'm right."

Ike cupped her fist in his big hand and pressed her fingers against his chest. For just a moment. Problem was, he liked her touch. He wanted more of it. And restraint had never been his strong suit.

He looked over her shoulder to the bed. In his mind's eye, he walked her backward toward it, his hands in her hair and his mouth claiming hers. Desire roared through him.

Shit. Time to fly.

"Listen, I haven't been up here for a while," Ike said, giving her hand a squeeze and then stepping away, breaking the contact. "I need to pick up some food for us. Any special requests?"

"Aw, look at you being all domestic," Jess said, a playful, ball-busting grin on her full red lips. "I'm seeing a whole other side of you."

Ike rolled his eyes, pretending like he didn't enjoy her taunting even though he did. Jess was fun and adventurous and the kind of woman who grabbed life with both hands and didn't let go. She played hard and loved freely, and he admired her for both. She didn't let other people's expectations run her life or set her agenda. She wore her heart on her face and in her eyes and on her skin. And she was brave and loyal, too—things that meant everything in his world. Those were core tenets of the code by which the Ravens lived and died.

"What-the-fuck-ever," Ike said, starting down the steps. He needed some distance from her. And he sure as hell needed to get his head on straight and his body under control. "Just some damn groceries. You have special requests or not?"

Her footsteps followed behind him. "I'll just go with you—"

"No," he said, his tone harsher than he'd intended. He turned to watch her make her way down.

Standing on the next-to-last step, Jess planted her hands on her curvy hips. Hips that would feel so damn good in *his* hands, provided he ever let himself off the leash where she was concerned. Which he hadn't. And wouldn't. "Why the hell not?" she asked, brown eyes flashing.

Shaking his head, Ike gave Jess's body a long, slow once-over, from her wavy red-streaked black hair, to the fucking luscious cleavage created by the red lace push-up bra she wore under the form-fitting black V-neck shirt, to the knee-high Goth boots she wore over a pair of torn-up black jeans that wrapped around her thighs like a second skin. Against all the black, the color of the tattoos on her arms and chest stood out like sun breaking through the clouds.

That *his hands* had put a lot of that ink on her skin? Made him more possessive of her than he had any right to be.

"Can't chance having the wrong person notice and identify you. You don't exactly blend in to the crowd." Understatement of the year, right there.

She smirked. "I can tone it down when the situation calls for it."

Ike immediately hated the thought. Jess was loud, vivid Technicolor in an in-your-face kinda way. Exactly the way it should be. "Not a chance. You could shave your head and wear a paper bag and I'd still know exactly who you were from a football field away."

"Ooh, kinky." Her smirk slid into a sexy grin.

Her word choice sent Ike's brain to all kinds of places it didn't need to be. Like envisioning Jess ass-up over his bike wearing only her ink and a pair of heels while he buried himself deep from behind, or imagining Jess with a ball gag taming that smart-ass mouth of hers while he made her come with his mouth and cock until she was boneless and more satisfied than she'd even been in her life. With black fastening straps and a red ball, the gag would match her hair. Something about that image pleased him greatly. And proved he'd fantasized about it a few times before today. Okay, a few thousand times. Whatever.

Did he always have to be so fucking attracted to women in trouble? Because he wasn't any fucking white knight, that was for damn sure. Cop father and friends, drug-addict-cop-killing friends, stalkerish ex-lovers who wanted more—Jess had been in one form of trouble or another for as long as Ike had known her. "Special requests or not, Jakes? Jesus Christmas."

She laughed, and Ike tried to ignore the way it lit him up inside. Despite her size, Jess had a big belly laugh so infectious it could make you chuckle even if you weren't in on the joke. Sometimes it even included snorts that would set her off laughing even harder. "You're too easy to rile up," she said through her laughter. Finally, she calmed enough to add, "Okay, okay. I'll be serious. Let's see…I'd love it if you could get iced blueberry Pop-Tarts or Lucky Charms for breakfast, and, like, pepperoni pizza Hot Pockets for lunch and dinner. Oh, and diet Coke. That would be awesome."

Ike frowned. "Anything else?"

Her eyes went distant for a second and then wide with excitement. "Oh, Doritos, too, please. Might need a couple of bags."

"Why do I feel like I'm talking to a nineteen-year-old frat boy right now?" he asked.

"Dude, you asked what I wanted. I can't help my junk food proclivities. I'm a terrible cook and Hot Pockets are freaking good. But wait. How are you going to get all that on the bike?"

Ike shook his head and pulled a key ring from his pocket. "I'm not. I've got a truck in the garage."

"Oh, okay. Well, I really would come help."

"I know you would. Just stay put. I won't be gone long. Use the house phone if you need me." He pointed toward the end of the kitchen counter, where the handset for the landline sat.

"I will," she said quietly, looking over her shoulder toward the phone.

Something about her tone made Ike pause, despite the fact that he could really use a breather from the sexual tension that always seemed to crackle between them no matter how unaffected he tried to act. "You okay being alone?"

Jess made a face. "Of course. You don't have to worry about me."

If only it was that easy. Especially when he could've lost her not twenty-four hours before. He might not want her for himself—no, that wasn't quite true, was it? He wanted her. He'd *always* wanted her. But he couldn't let himself have her because he'd never be able to give her all of him. Jess deserved a whole man. And Ike hadn't been whole for almost eighteen years, when a part of him had died along with the first woman he'd ever loved.

And that wanting? That's why he needed to get the hell out of this house for a while. He turned on his heel. "Remember the rules," he said over his shoulder. "And lock the door behind me."

"Aye, aye, captain," Jess said, the snark back in full force. Then Ike was out the door. "Don't forget the Doritos. Lots and lots of Doritos," he heard as he closed it behind him. Fucking Doritos.

Ike walked his bike back toward the garage—no need to advertise his presence here. Except for the Hard Ink team and the Ravens' club president, Dare Kenyon, no one else knew where Ike and Jess had gone. And Ike was happy keeping it that way for now. He even planned to go to a store on the edge of Frederick instead of the more convenient one that was only a few miles from the club's compound.

He parked the Harley on the side of the garage and then unlocked the side door to the small one-car-wide building. The black and silver 1975 Ford F-250 gleamed where the sunlight streaked through the door and onto the steel and chrome. Ike had restored it a decade before and it was in pristine condition.

He was for shit at taking care of people, but he could take care of machines on wheels like nobody's business.

Enough, he thought, slamming the truck's door harder than necessary.

Enough thinking about the past. About how he couldn't save Lana. About wanting Jess and not being able to have her.

He had a job to do and that was all that mattered. *Jess* was all that mattered. Keeping her alive until the clusterfuck with Nick's Special Forces team was resolved once and for all. Until Nick's enemies no longer posed Jess any threat for being able to identify who at least one of them was. That was what Ike's brain needed to be focused on. And nothing else.

For fuck's sake.

The moment he turned out of his driveway and onto the road, an unwelcome anxiety settled into his gut. He didn't like leaving Jess alone. But he'd only be gone for an hour. Even Jess could keep herself out of trouble for that long.

Chapter 3

Jess watched Ike walk out the door, all the while keeping her *Fine, fine, I'm totally fine* expression plastered on her face. The moment he was gone, her shoulders sagged under the weight of being alone in a strange place not that many hours after strange men had proven that not even familiar places were safe.

Stop it, Jess. You are *fine. Or, at least, you can fake it until you make it.*

She nodded to herself. Had plenty of experience doing that, didn't she?

Step one was locking herself in nice and tight, so Jess crossed the room and threw all three locks.

Standing with her back to the door, she surveyed the cabin, wondering what to do with herself next. She sank into the couch and turned on the TV. Daytime television pretty much sucked ass, though, and it was amazing that so many channels existed and yet almost all of them were filled with crap. She paused on a house hunting show she liked but the husband wanted absolutely ridiculous things including a skateboarding park in the backyard. Like, an actual skateboarding park. So she turned the idiot box off and dropped the remote onto the cushion next to her.

At a loss for what to do, she wandered into the kitchen and got a glass of water. The breeze coming through the windows was fresh and fragrant, like flowers and pine needles. Clearly, she wasn't in downtown Baltimore anymore.

Turning, her gaze fell on the duffle she'd quickly packed in the middle of the night. She'd been so shaken and anxious to hurry, she wasn't even sure what the hell she'd thrown in the bag. For all she knew she had twenty panties and no pants. Which would make things really interesting around here if it were true…

Jess smirked and put her glass in the sink.

She carried the duffle to the bathroom and unpacked her toiletries and makeup, and then she went up to the loft to put away her clothes. Ah, damn, she had in fact brought pants. And shirts, too. No parading around naked to drive Ike crazy, after all.

Warm air hung in the loft like a wool blanket, so Jess turned on the ceiling fan and opened the room's only window, which overlooked a small backyard that sloped downward toward the woods. Not too far off, she could see the lake she'd noticed when they'd first turned on to Ike's property. It was weird to think of Ike in a place like this when almost all of Jess's associations of him were at Hard Ink, a tattoo parlor in a gritty and largely abandoned industrial area in Baltimore.

Turning away from the window, she couldn't help but focus on the bed—the most prominent piece in the room. A hunter-green comforter covered it, and four pillows with green-and-blue-striped cases sat piled at the top of the bed. The idea of Ike sacking out on the couch still didn't sit right with Jess, who wasn't sure how much more sacrifice on her behalf she could take from the guy. But the feeling of being a burden was a dear old frenemy she didn't have a prayer of shaking any time soon.

Sighing, she emptied her bag onto the bed. Among the pants, shirts, sleep shorts, tank tops, and underthings, she found a strappy little red dress. *Why* she'd brought a dress, she had no idea. In her haste to grab and go, she'd mostly pulled things out of a basket of folded laundry sitting on her bedroom floor, not realizing it was among them. The closet was pretty full of Ike's clothing, but Jess managed to find a free hanger for the dress. She stared at it sandwiched between a steel gray button-down and an old, frayed sweatshirt. It was stupid, but she liked seeing her clothes comingled with Ike's…

Ugh, Jess. Now you're *the one being ridiculous.* Only, unlike the TV, she couldn't simply press a button to get away from all the crap in her own head.

The sound of kids screaming and laughing echoed up from the lake and pulled her out of the inane thoughts. It was a sound of such pure innocence that it simultaneously made Jess smile and tear up. Despite the fact that her mother had run off when she was eight, Jess's dad had been *awesome*. He'd been busy as hell as a Baltimore police detective, but he was always attentive and funny and loving. He'd bought her first hair dye kit and gotten his fingers all stained purple helping her do it. He'd taken her dress shopping for proms and homecomings, and never said a word that her fashion choices trended toward combat boots and skulls. He'd given her an amazing childhood, and the laughter made her think of him. And miss him. And feel guilty all over again. Because he'd been killed four years ago. Protecting her.

Just like Ike was doing now. And the situation was equally—if not more—dangerous. Jess shivered.

More screams from the lake. Except…

Awareness shot through Jess and chased away the haze of memories and the tangle of troubled thoughts. Someone was screaming…and it sounded different now. Not playful, but panicked. She ducked her head into the opening in the window…and heard a faint but very clear shout for help.

Jess's scalp prickled and a chill ran down her back.

One moment, she stood paralyzed, and the next she was barreling down the steps, through the kitchen, and out the back door. She paused in the backyard long enough to hear more desperate cries and spotted a trail that cut into the woods from behind Ike's garage. Jess made a beeline for it, stopping every so often to make sure she was still headed in the direction of whoever was in trouble.

It seemed like she was running down a hallway that just keep getting longer and longer, but eventually the trail turned and opened up, providing a straight-on view of the water. Sweating and breathing hard, Jess broke through the edge of the trees and skidded to a halt. Scanning the lake, she saw someone splashing and trying to hold onto what appeared to be a small, overturned boat. Cries also came from a dock a little ways around the lake, where a lady was calling out to the person in the water. Jess took off toward her.

The woman noticed Jess first and flung an arm over her head. As Jess got closer, she noticed that the woman was older, her braided, pale-blonde hair all shot through with gray. In jeans and a white blouse, she was also pretty, and she reminded Jess of an old-time country-western star. A lawn chair sat behind where she stood on the dock.

"Can you swim?" the woman called, her voice strained with fear. "I can't and my little guy can't either, and I'm afraid Ben's gonna pull Sam under trying to keep himself above water. I've called my husband but I don't know how long it'll take him to get here. Oh, God." The words spilled out in a jumbled rush.

Jess's boots pounded on the wooden planks as she closed the distance between her and the lady. "I can swim," Jess said. "How deep is it?" She bent to unzip her tall boots and inhaled deeply, trying to get her breathing under control.

"Oh, I'm not sure. Not too deep here, but deep enough out there that they won't have a chance of touching." The woman paced, her hand against her forehead to shield her eyes from the sun. "Hang on, Sam!"

The minute both boots were off, Jess climbed down the metal ladder at the end of the dock. The dark-green water immediately soaked through her jeans, much colder than she expected given the warm day. Fuck, she should've taken the denim off, too, but it was too late to worry about that now.

"Oh, hurry!" the lady cried.

Jess pushed off with her feet against one of the slimy wooden pylons and swam as fast as she could. That it had been a *long* time since the last time she'd gone swimming was immediately clear, but she couldn't worry about that right now. She couldn't worry about the bite of the cold water or the drag of the heavy denim or that she was already tired from the uncharacteristic run from Ike's house—not to mention the fact that she'd only gotten about two hours sleep before the noise of someone breaking into her house had sent her scurrying for a hiding place.

Legs kicking, arms plowing into the water, Jess pushed herself for long minutes until finally, *finally* she was close enough to talk to the boys.

"Hey guys," she said in a breathy voice. "I'm Jess."

"I'm Sam," the bigger boy said, fingers gripped around a handle on the edge of the boat. "This is Ben," Sam said. Crying, the little boy stared at her with wide, terrified eyes, his arms wrapped tightly around the other boy's neck.

"Hi, Sam." She swam closer, close enough that her hand grasped at the boat's aluminum bottom. "Ben. Do you think you can—"

The little boy dove at her and clutched her around the neck. His legs wrapped around her belly like a vise.

Unprepared for the extra weight, she nearly went under. Jess grasped the same handle onto which Sam hung, pulled herself up, and shook the water off her face. Ben wailed into her ear. She had to get him calmed if she had any chance of getting him back to shore. She rubbed small circles against his back. "It's okay, Ben. I've got you. I'm gonna give you a tow back to the dock, okay? But I need you to calm down first."

"I caaaan't," the boy cried.

"He thinks he saw a snake after we flipped the boat," Sam said.

Oh, fuck. Snakes were great as tattoos and jewelry. In real life, not so much. Jess schooled her expression and forced a smile. "Even if you did, he's long gone by now. All the noise we're making would totally scare him away." Hopefully. Please, God.

Ben's crying turned into a breathy whimper. "Weally?"

"Really," Jess said. "And if you could stop crying, I bet it would make the lady on the dock feel a lot better. She's really worried, and now that I'm here, there's nothing to worry about. Right?"

"G'amma's worried?" Ben asked, his breath hitching as he looked over her shoulder.

"She is, but it's all okay now. Right?" Jess continued to rub circles against the boy's back and, slowly but surely, his breathing evened out and slowed down. Finally, he heaved a big, tired-sounding sigh. "You ready?"

"I dunno," he said, fear plain in his voice.

"I'm gonna do all the work. All you have to do is hold on to my arm," she said. "Can I show you how we'll do it?" Just when she was sure Ben was going to refuse, he nodded. "Okay, great. You're being really brave, Ben. I'm gonna turn you around and hold your back to my front. But I promise I'm not gonna let go."

"Promise?" he said, the strain of tears returning to his voice.

"I totally promise." Jess hooked her arm around his neck and across his chest, her hand finding a hold under his arm. She hadn't used her teenage lifeguard training in years, but when she was younger, she used to love to swim. Of course, after her dad died, she no longer had access to his gym, and Jess had sorta let the swimming go...along with so much else. When Ben finally relaxed against her again, she shook away the thoughts and looked at Sam. "Will you be okay while I take him back?"

"I can swim back myself," Sam said.

"Are you sure?"

He looked toward the shore, the doubt clear in his eyes.

"I'll come right back for you, Sam. You were holding Ben up all this time, so you've got to be tired." Jess ignored her own growing exhaustion. *Suck it up, buttercup.*

"O-okay," Sam finally said. "I'll wait."

"Good man. All right, Ben. Here we go, nice and easy, okay?" She lay back in the water, using her free arm and her legs to propel them shoreward. It was slow going, to be sure. Jess's lungs burned and her shoulder muscles felt like Jell-O. Ben whimpered and sniffled and occasionally lifted his head to see how far they'd gone, but Jess was impressed by how he'd managed to calm himself down. He really was a brave kid. They both were.

When Jess had nearly reached the dock, the low *whirr* of an engine reached her through the sounds of her own splashing and heavy breathing, but she couldn't divert even a moment's worth of energy away from getting Ben to safety. As it was, she was already starting to worry about how she'd get Sam in, too. But one thing at a time.

The aluminum of the ladder against her palm felt like the biggest victory ever. "Here we go, Ben," she said.

"Oh, thank goodness." Ben's grandmother extended a hand down to the little boy.

"Don't worry, G'amma," he said, clutching the metal and hauling himself up.

The woman laughed and hugged the boy into her arms, getting herself soaked in the process. It didn't look like she minded one bit.

"Okay," Jess said, clutching the ladder with cold fingers. "I'll go get Sam now." Heaving a deep breath, she pushed off the dock.

"Wait," the grandmother said. "That's my husband and Doc coming."

A few feet out, Jess treaded water, her gaze scanning for the incoming boat. Sure enough, a small motorboat was making its way toward the overturned rowboat. The older woman yelled and gestured, and Sam swam around the end and waved until one of the men waved back.

Jess looked up at the other woman. "I'll still go out if you think I should."

"No, hon. You've done enough. Come on out of there now."

With a glance back at Sam, Jess returned to the dock. Climbing the ladder took way more effort than it probably should've, but she forced herself up and out of the water until she was finally standing. A puddle of water formed all around her bare, ice-cold feet.

As they stood watching, the motorboat pulled up along Sam. One of the men hauled him out of the water and wrapped him in a towel, and then it took both of the men to right the rowboat. They slid it alongside them and slowly towed it back to shore.

The older woman put her arm around Jess's shoulders and hugged her in. "I can't thank you enough. I'm Bernie, by the way, but everyone calls me Bunny."

"You're welcome, Bunny. I'm Jess," she answered, and then she mentally kicked herself for revealing her real name. Maybe it didn't matter, or maybe it did. Either way, *that* was the exact moment it occurred to Jess that she'd pretty much broken every one of Ike's rules in about a fifteen-minute time span.

Oh, shit.

Chapter 4

Ike unlocked the front door then scooped up the bags of groceries he'd dropped at his feet. Hands full, he made his way inside and headed straight for the kitchen.

"Yo, Jess. I'm back," he called, settling the bags on the counter. He inhaled to call her name again when he noticed something that shot ice through his veins—the back door stood open. "Fuck!" He darted out the door and onto the small back porch, but the yard was empty. "Jess!" he shouted. "Jessica!"

Sonofafuck.

Ike didn't know whether to be terrified that something had happened to her or angry that she'd left the house, and the combination of both emotions flowing through him was like a noxious, dangerous cocktail that had taken him from sober to fucked up in two point five seconds.

He tore back into the house and hauled ass up the loft stairs—just to be sure. Empty. As was the rest of the house. On the back porch again, his brain raced as his eyes scanned. The only thing back there was the trail to the lake.

The low growl of a motorboat's engine sounded in the distance. And though it was probably a ridiculous reaction, dread settled over Ike like a second skin, but he was too used to worst-case scenarios actually coming true.

His feet were in motion before he'd made the conscious decision to move. Partway down the trail, the surface smoothed out to mostly dirt, and that was when Ike noticed the shoe prints. He slowed to a walk. Just one set. Small foot size. Which meant... He was gonna kill her. He really fucking was. Right after he pulled her into his arms and made sure she was okay.

Ike ran the rest of the way into the clearing, his gaze quickly settling on a grouping of people down at the Aldersons' old dock. And there, in the middle of the group, was a very petite woman with black hair wearing all black.

That was his girl.

Well, not his.

Whatthefuckever.

He took off in the direction of the dock. Before he even got there, he made out the identity of the others—Doc, Rodeo, Bunny, Sam, and Ben—all members of the Ravens' family in one way or another. Ike's brain scrambled for a rational explanation for the scene in front of him, but he was too fucking angry and worried and worked the hell up. Rational might as well have been a foreign country.

"Hey, Ike," Doc called, giving a wave from where he stood at the end of the pier. Tall and wiry, Frank "Doc" Kenyon had shoulder-length white-gray hair on his head and his face. He was the club president's grandfather and half-owner of the compound that included the Ravens' clubhouse and the racetrack. Dare Kenyon, the club prez and Ike's good friend, owned the other half and would inherit everything when Doc decided he was done with this world and everyone in it. Some days, that seemed like it might happen sooner rather than later because the old man's hip and knee replacement a few years back gave him all kinds of difficulties and—worst of all—kept him from riding much anymore. Ike was pretty sure he'd want to go before reaching that day, so he couldn't really blame the guy.

Ike slowed to a walk as his boots hit the wooden planks. He held his hand toward Doc's but his eyes were all for Jess…who was soaking wet. What in the ever-living hell? "Doc," he said, giving the older man a quick handshake. He moved past Doc just as quick. "Hey, Ike, wait…"

But the roar between Ike's ears was too loud for listening. He marched right into the group of people crowded around the end of the dock and bore down on Jess. Clipped, angry words spilled out of him. "You want to tell me why you're down here? You know, given the motherfu—" He swallowed the curse word when he noticed Ben's wide eyes staring up at him. "Given the situation and our conversation earlier?"

The sum total of Jess's initial reaction was a single eyebrow lifting into an arch. Just the left one. The movement made him take in the droplets of water trailing down her face from her wavy, wet hair, the smudges of mascara below her lashes, and the shiver of her lower lip. Finally, she said, "I had a good reason."

"*Jessica—*"

"Ike, honey," Bunny said, smiling. Despite being in her sixties, Doc's sister still had her looks—and plenty of sass. "Your Jessica was a total heroine just now. So slow your roll before you say something you regret. Besides, Dare called earlier to let us know you were bringing someone up here for protection. So don't worry. Jess didn't spill any beans."

Amusement spilled into Jess's brown eyes, and then she chuckled. "Bunny, I think you might be one of my favorite people, like, ever."

Bunny put her arm around Jess's shoulder and hugged her in. "Us old ladies got to stick together."

Old ladies? Oh, for fuck sake. Ike wasn't sure he could ever see himself making that leap, and certainly not with Jessica "I can indeed find trouble in less than an hour" Jakes.

A headache bloomed behind Ike's eyes as he looked between the two women, and then to Doc and Rodeo, Bunny's second husband whose son Slider was Ben and Sam's dad. The two other men stared back at him with a mixture of amusement and sympathy.

Ike threw out his hands. "Could someone please explain what the hel— heck happened here?"

"Miss Jess rescued Ben and me after we flipped the rowboat," Sam said, his shaggy dark-brown hair and green eyes so much like his father's. "Or, at least, she would've rescued me, too, if Doc and Pop hadn't shown up first. But she got Ben back before he completely freaked out and drowned me while he was at it."

"Did not freak out," Ben said.

"Did, too," Sam said.

Ike ground the heel of his hand into his eye, a vain attempt to relieve the throbbing there. The story still didn't make much sense to him, but if what Slider's boy said was true, what Jess had done was big. The only thing the club valued as much as taking care of its own was taking care of those who couldn't take care of themselves.

"I heard them screaming for help from the house," Jess said. "I should've thought twice about running down here, but I…" She shrugged, then shivered. "I just acted."

Ike gave a tight nod. Her words took the edge off of his anger, although his insides were still keyed up from the fear-based adrenaline flooding through him. Not to mention, the more people who knew Jess was here, the more Ike worried that a single unintentional slip could put her in danger. Again. Of course, everyone here knew that the club had allied itself with Nick and his friends—an alliance that Ike had helped broker given his close relationship with both. And certainly everyone understood what was at stake, especially after an enemy attack on the Hard Ink building had collapsed part of the roof on the large L-shaped building and killed Harvey and Creed, two of their members, two of their brothers. So it wasn't a question of any of these people putting Jess in danger knowingly. But Ike couldn't be too careful, not where Jess was concerned. Not given how lethal the mercenaries were that the Ravens and Hard Ink team had been fighting.

Ike heaved a deep breath. "You boys okay now?" he asked, looking between Sam and Ben. They both nodded, and then turned to thank and hug Jess. Ike watched as she interacted with the kids, her behavior so natural and comfortable with them. And it did something…funny to him. Made him think. Made him wonder. Made him want.

And it certainly made him look at Jess in a whole new way—and not just because his mind was playing with the image of her belly rounding with a child. Okay, *his* child. But because she'd risked herself for someone else's kids. Given everything Slider had already lost, Ike knew how much those boys meant to the guy, which meant what Jess had done was going to mean a lot to him, too.

Bunny was right. Jess was a hero.

"Well, we'll get 'em back home now," Rodeo said, waving the boys into the motorboat.

Ike nodded. "Roger that."

Bunny stepped in front of Jess and wrapped the younger woman up in a big hug. "You ever need a *thing*, don't hesitate to ask. I owe you, Jess."

"It was nothing. Really. I'm glad I could help," Jess said, her voice subdued, not to mention a little shaky.

Bunny shook her head. "It wasn't nothing to me." As Jess nodded, the older woman gave her husband a kiss. "My car is up at the Alderson's old place. I'll meet you back at home."

With longish gray hair and a beard, Rodeo always half looked like he was smiling, but never more than when he was with Bunny. "All right, darlin'." She reached for a lawn chair sitting on the dock and he put his hand on it. "I got this." Bunny gave him another kiss and took off.

Doc limped toward Ike and clapped him on the shoulder. "Good to have you back in our neck of the woods, Ike. Can't wait 'til everyone's back."

"Me, too," Ike said. Because it would mean that the war someone was waging against his friends—and now his club—would be over. Once and for all. "Thanks, Doc."

"Don't thank me. Thank your little lady." Doc winked at Jess, earning him a smile from her.

And then they were all in the boat and easing away from the dock, the boys' rowboat tied behind them. Ike returned a few waves and then turned to Jess.

"You're pissed," she said. "Ike, I'm—"

Without a word and without warning, Ike grabbed Jess around the thighs and heaved her body over his shoulder, lifting her into a fireman's carry. He retreated down the dock, scooping up her boots as he went, and ignoring the fuck out of the hooting and hollering he was pretty sure he heard from his friends in the boat.

"Oh, my God, you cretin! Put me down!" She beat her fists against his back and kicked her feet.

Ike used his other arm to still her legs. "No."

"Ike, what the fuck? I don't freaking need you to carry me," Jess yelled, using her arms to try to push her body up.

"Too bad. I need to carry you," he said. He regretted the admission but couldn't deny the truth of the words. He *needed* her in his arms. He needed the proof of life.

"But your big-ass shoulder is in my gut and I'm probably going to puke all over you," she said, apparently not impressed by his words.

"No you won't."

"Oh. Well, if you say so. For fuck's sake." She kept up a steady stream of grumbling the whole way home, but it didn't bother Ike one bit. Because she was warm and whole and safe in his arms.

Finally, he climbed the steps to the back porch and carried Jess into the kitchen. He secured the door, then slowly lowered her to her feet to stand against the wall behind the door. He braced his hands on either side of her, boxing her in, forcing them close, making her see him, *hear* him. He ought to walk away, clear his head, get himself under control. But he couldn't force the distance between them, no matter how much he should.

He bent down, way down, so that his eyes were aligned with hers. "That's the second time in twenty-four hours that you've scared the fuck out of me," he said, nailing her with a stare.

For a long moment, her expression was filled with uncertainty and confusion, and then her gaze dragged down his face and settled on his lips. She licked her own, and Ike couldn't help but track the movement and want to warm her body up with his—starting with that sweet, smart little mouth. "I didn't mean to. Either time," she said.

He just stared at her, his head too tangled up to articulate all the things he wanted to say—and to figure out which of those he absolutely shouldn't say. Ever. Because he understood enough about himself to realize that he was this wound up for a reason. He cared about Jess. A lot. And if things were different... *But they're fucking not.*

Right.

Suddenly, Jess's cold hands were on his cheeks. Where her touch was tentative, her eyes were filled with heat...and challenge. "Kiss me," she whispered as she slowly leaned in.

"Don't," he said.

"Why not?" she asked, so close now that her breath caressed his skin.

Yeah, why not? Traitorous brain.

She ghosted her lips over his, mimicking the act of kissing while purposely keeping a hair's breadth between them. Ike's blood flashed hot and his cock was instantly rigid in his jeans. "Taste me," she whispered.

Fuck, he wanted to. He wanted to kiss her and penetrate her and claim her. In any and every way.

Ike forced himself back. The space unleashed an ache inside his chest—but better a little pain now than a lot later. That was a lesson he'd learned over and over. "I need to keep my eyes on the prize, Jessica. And that's you, safe." He scrubbed his hands over his face. "I'll, uh, I'll get you a towel."

Chapter 5

What the hell just happened?

Still pinned to the kitchen wall, Jess watched Ike walk away. Twin reactions roared through her—hurt at his rejection, and appreciation for the fact that he wanted to take care of her. At least he hadn't been as mad at her as she thought he'd be—well, once he understood why she'd left, that was. She probably should've thought about what she was doing when she went flying out of the house—not to mention what Ike would think about it. But, damnit, she was her father's daughter, and there was absolutely no way she could hear someone in need and stand by without helping.

Ike, of all people, had to understand that.

"Here," he said, returning with a big beige towel.

"Thanks." She grasped the terry cloth. He didn't let go of it right away, and it made her look up to his face—where she found his dark eyes absolutely blazing down at her. Jess didn't think she was imagining the raw need she saw there, especially when she finally dropped her gaze only to find herself staring at a prominent bulge in the front of his jeans.

Holy shit!

Abruptly, Ike turned away and busied himself at the counter.

Dazed with lust and confusion, Jess scrubbed the towel over her face and hair and then wrapped it around her shoulders. The dry warmth of the cloth made her realize how chilly she was in the wet clothes. "I think I'll take a shower," she said. "Warm up."

Ike nodded. "Good. I've gotta get the rest of the groceries from the truck."

As he made for the front door, Jess retreated into the bathroom and quietly closed herself in. For a long moment, she just stood there, back to the cool wood. And then something occurred to her. Ike hadn't said he didn't want to kiss her, or even that they shouldn't. He hadn't really rejected her, had he?

Or maybe she was reading into her memory of the moment what she wanted to see.

Probably.

Then again, he'd been hard. And he'd looked at her like he wanted to eat her. And she was totally game to be his buffet.

She knocked her head against the door. Twice, for good measure. Because it didn't matter how much his body reacted if his brain was telling him to stay away.

Crap. How long were they going to be trapped here together? Because being so close to what she wanted twenty-four/seven but not being allowed to have it was going to suck ass. Big time.

Jess lingered in the shower longer than strictly necessary, but the warm water felt so good on her sore, tired muscles that she couldn't force herself out. By the time she toweled off, she was yawning and her limbs felt like they'd gained twenty pounds each. She hung her wet clothes over the shower curtain bar and secured the towel around her torso. Being upright was nearly painful after so many hours awake, so Jess could do little more than stumble out of the bathroom.

She walked right into a wall of strong, hard muscle that woke her right up.

"Oh. Ike. Sorry. What are you doing?" she asked, stepping back. Arms crossed in a way that highlighted the thick mounds of his biceps, Ike was leaning against the jamb, his broad shoulders covering most of the doorway. Like he'd been waiting for her to come out.

"I handled that all wrong," he said.

Jess blinked, her brain scrambling to figure out which "that" he was talking about. The scent of him, all masculine spice and summer air, didn't help, either. *God*, she wanted him. "Uh, handled what all wrong?" she managed.

"What you did…Doc was right. I should've thanked you, not yelled at you. Fuck, Jess." He nailed her with a stare nearly as intense as the one he'd given her in the kitchen. Though, where that one had been full of heat, this one seemed softer…affectionate? Or was that more projecting? "Those boys mean the world to Slider. I owe you."

She sighed. "Ike, you're putting your whole life on hold for me.

You totally do not owe me anything. And I understand why you were worried. I should've let you know where I'd gone. Oh, well, I guess I don't know how I would've done that without my cell, but, anyway, I get it."

He pulled something from his pocket. Her phone. "That's why I'm giving you this back. I should've trusted you to not use it unless it's an emergency. And that way, I can reach you, too."

Jess accepted the phone into her hand and nodded. "Thanks."

And then they just stared at each for a long moment. Jess went from feeling amused to awkward to observed...and that made her hot. Especially as she was standing there in nothing but a towel.

As if he could hear her thoughts, Ike's gaze slowly ran down her neck to her chest. She wiped at something there and the wetness on the fingers told her it had been a droplet of water from her hair. Ike watched the movement of her hand openly, hungrily, and his desire made her bold, daring, hungry in return.

Without giving herself time to second-guess the idea, she reached out and lightly dragged her wet fingers against his bottom lip.

And it was like she'd unleashed a beast.

Ike grabbed her wrist and hauled her to him. He was on her everywhere. His hands in her hair, on her back, grabbing her ass and lifting her up so that her legs circled his hips. His tongue licked the exact route that water droplet had taken, from chest to neck to ear. And then he was kissing her, fucking her mouth with his tongue, absolutely devouring her.

Jess held on like her life depended on it, and at some point she became aware of the breeze on her bare skin. She'd dropped the towel, which meant she was totally buck-ass naked in Ike's big arms, and she couldn't have cared less.

Ike licked her mouth, sucked her tongue, nipped at her lips. He turned with her still in his arms and made for the stairs, and Jess thought she might die from sheer joy and anticipation. He tasted like strength and sin and sex, and she tightened her legs around his hips as he carried her to the loft, eager to see if *all* of him tasted so good—or even better.

When they reached the second floor, Ike growled low in his throat and his grip tightened on her ass, his fingers digging in. She moaned and—

Cool air from the ceiling fan washed over Jess as Ike dropped her onto the bed—and promptly turned around to leave. Jess was so stunned she couldn't speak. Just as he hit the top of the steps, he said, "Don't fucking tease me, Jessica. I'm trying to do right by you, but I'm still just a goddamned man."

* * * *

Ike felt like a bomb waiting to go off.

For one goddamned second, he'd let himself off the leash, and he'd been all over Jess.

For two glorious minutes, he'd held her and tasted her and had his hands and mouth all over her.

For the past three hours, he'd worn a path in the wooden floor of his cabin, wanting more but holding himself back from taking it. And feeling hungry and empty and desperate, like a man who'd just had his last meal and would now be forced to go without for the rest of his life.

After the stunt he'd pulled, he was also worried about Jess. Because after he'd dropped her curvy little ass on the bed—trying like hell not to put a visual to the fucking incredible physical sensations he had from carrying her naked body up the stairs, she'd never come back down.

She hadn't said a word or made a sound, either. And combined with the chaos roaring through Ike's body, her silence was driving him stark-raving mad.

Man-up, Ike. You created this problem. Fucking fix it.

He walked to the bottom of the steps. "Jess?" No answer. "Jess, I'm coming up." Nothing. He frowned, but then he was in motion, his boots thudding against the treads as he made his way to the loft.

The sight that greeted him sucker-punched him right in the heart.

Jess was curled into a little ball on her side, her hands tucked under her face. She'd folded the blanket over her, but it had slid down, leaving her shoulder and breasts exposed.

God, she was fucking beautiful.

Maybe it made him a pervert, but Ike was drawn to the bed. He crouched down beside it, his gaze drinking Jess in. Her skin was a work of art. Her right arm had a swirling watercolor rainbow and waterfall running the whole length of it, flowers and fish woven in. Her shoulder and biceps had an ornate Mexican *calavera* skull, the detail done in reds and golds and dark blues. Ike remembered every one of the after-hours sessions they'd spent together doing these pieces, Jess telling him one colorful story after another. The time with her had made it simultaneously easier and harder to go home to his empty apartment—

easier because her liveliness and passion filled up some of the dark, lonely places inside him; harder because he never felt more empty and alone in his apartment than after spending a night with Jess talking his ear off. Smiling at him. Teasing him. Making him want.

On her other arm, Ike could just make out the black and dark-green leaves surrounding the wide-open faces of a half-dozen bright-pink roses. She'd already had part of that sleeve done when Ike first met her, but he'd expanded it for her over the years.

His gaze skimmed over her chest, where a constellation of different sized dark-blue and black nautical stars spilled over her right collarbone, down her chest, between the curves of her breasts, to finally end in a sweeping flourish on the right side of her ribs. She was fascinating and alluring to look at, and that was saying absolutely nothing about the little silver hoops piercing through her nipples. Jesus.

Ike reached across Jess and pulled up the blanket, covering her.

What was even more fascinating, though, was her face. Usually so animated, colorful, and just fucking *alive* with emotion, she looked peaceful and oddly young sleeping, her face bare of makeup. And it made him feel even more protective of her.

With gentle fingers, he pushed a wave of black and red hair off her face—and was surprised to feel how warm her cheek felt. He pressed his fingers to her forehead and found her warm there, too. Someday he'd get around to installing air conditioning in this old place, but he spent so much more of his time in Baltimore that he hadn't made it a priority.

Sighing, Ike made his way back downstairs. At least she hadn't come back down because she was avoiding him. And now that he thought about it, he was fucking tired, too. Jess had called him around four in the morning and he'd made it to her apartment on the second floor of an old row house within twenty minutes. After he'd gotten her out of that little shit hole of a crawl space and held her in his arms to prove to himself he hadn't lost her, they'd packed a bag, gone back to his apartment so he could pack and grab some extra firepower, and made their way to the remaining part of the Hard Ink building in time for the team's morning brief about their investigation.

He kicked off his boots and stretched out on the couch, intent on catching a little shut-eye himself. Except the minute his eyes closed, a movie started playing on the back of his lids. The terrified and embarrassed look on Jess's face during that morning brief when she saw the projected image of a tattoo worn by one of their enemies—and she realized she'd slept with someone wearing a tat just like that a few days before.

His eyes blinked open again and his gaze settled on the ceiling's exposed wooden beams.

Given the way Ike had always felt about Jess, he didn't love hearing about her sexual exploits—which were many and often colorful. Not because he disapproved, but because he wished he could be the one making her come, making her shake, making her scream his name. Otherwise, he didn't get a fucking say in who Jess gave her love or her body to, and he knew it.

But Ike did get to be pissed that someone had apparently picked her up for the express purpose of using her for information about Nick and Jeremy, and then came back days later, after attacking and destroying part of Hard Ink, to tie up loose ends. As if Jess was just so much disposable trash.

Ike's hands fisted.

The only thing he hated about protecting Jess right now was that it kept him from being a part of the fight back in Baltimore...where Ike might get the hands-on opportunity to find the man who had done these things to Jess and teach him some manners—or put him in the grave. Ike didn't really care which.

Ike wasn't aware of finally drifting off to sleep. All he knew was that he opened his eyes to total darkness. He flew into a sitting position. Momentarily forgetting where he was, he reached for the lamp on the nightstand that wasn't there. Because he wasn't in his apartment back home, he was at the cabin. With Jess.

How the hell long had he been asleep?

He reached for the lamp on the console table behind him and flicked it on.

Across the room, the kitchen clock hanging on the wall said it was almost nine thirty. Jesus, he'd slept all day.

On a big yawn, Ike rubbed the heels of his hands against his eyes, and then he heaved himself off the couch. His eyes went immediately to the loft, which was as quiet and still as it'd been earlier in the day.

"Jess?" he called. Nothing. And then...was that a small moan? He crossed to the steps. "Jessica, you up?"

"Ike," she said in a croaking voice.

Ike took the steps two at a time and found Jess lying on her back. In the dim light cast by the lamp downstairs, he could see that she'd pushed the covers down below her belly button. As he closed the distance between them, she pulled a pillow over her breasts, and the movement looked like it took an inordinate amount of effort.

Ike frowned and sat on the edge of the bed. Before he even touched her, he could feel the heat radiating off of her. And it had nothing to do with the lack of air conditioning in the cabin because the night air had cooled the place down by a lot. "Hey. You okay?"

She shook her head. "Feel bad."

He put his hand on her forehead. Her skin was on fire. "Jesus, you're burning up."

Jess grasped his hand in both of hers and pressed it more firmly to her forehead, then her cheek, then her neck. "Hand is cold. Feels so good."

"Besides the fever, what else feels bad?" he asked.

"Just hurt everywhere," she said, looking up at him. The pain on her face and in her eyes slayed him.

"We need to break this fever. I'll be back."

She clung harder to his hand. "Don't leave."

He kissed her forehead. "I'm not. Just getting something to make you feel better."

"'kay," she whispered. As he rose, she turned onto her side, balling herself around the pillow. Drawing her knees up pulled them out from under the covers, exposing the big, intricate dream catcher that started on her hip and ran beaded feathers down the outside of her thigh.

Ike had done that piece, too.

God, it was like he could measure his life these past few years in the moments he spent putting ink on her body.

Downstairs, Ike made quick work of gathering some Ibuprofen, a glass of water, and a wet washcloth. When he returned, Jess was in the same position as when he'd left, her heavy eyelids making it clear she'd nearly fallen back to sleep.

He needed to get drugs in her first. "Hey, Jess. Can you wake up? I have some medicine for you."

She pushed herself onto an elbow and downed the pills and some water. "Thanks." When she settled down again, he placed the cold washcloth against her forehead. She moaned and covered it with her hand. "That feels good."

Ike nodded and cleared his throat. "You know, uh, you never got dressed before you fell asleep earlier. Want me to grab you a T-shirt? Or something?"

"Too hot," she whispered. "Is it bothering you?"

Given the amount of ink he'd put on her body, he'd seen *a lot* of her up close and personal—he'd done the stars running around her right breast, after all. And he knew how much it pleased her that he appreciated what he saw, too. So, under other circumstances, he might've suspected her of being coy, but there wasn't an ounce of mischief in her right now. "No. Just don't want to make you uncomfortable."

"Never could," she said, eyes drifting shut. "You're a good man, Ike Young. The best."

As much as he couldn't agree with the sentiment, he also couldn't deny liking hearing it. From her.

He grasped the washcloth to turn it over, only to feel it soaked through with the heat of her fever. This time when he left, she didn't notice. He cooled it down in the bathroom sink, then returned to her bedside and laid it against her forehead and the side of her face.

In her sleep, the corner of her mouth curved up.

Ike sat on the edge of the bed for a long while, and then he moved to the old brown armchair that sat in the corner by the window and pulled out his phone.

What's the word there? He shot off the text to Dare.

Dare's response popped up a minute later. *We set up some snipers' roosts to get better eyes on the area. Holed up in one for the night. Got the guys organized into watch units. Otherwise things are quiet.* Dare was a good choice for lookout—he was one of the best shots Ike knew.

Sorry I'm not there, Ike replied.

Do the job you need to do, Dare said. Of all people, Ike knew Dare wouldn't question his need to protect Jess. No one knew the full extent of the shit that had rained down on Dare as a kid, but the man seemed to have devoted his life to making up for it by taking care of as many people as he could. Hell, Dare had put it right there in the Ravens' motto: "Ride. Fight. Defend."

Another message from Dare: *Jeremy accepted responsibility for Harvey and Creed's deaths today.*

What the fuck? Why would Jeremy think he was responsible for the Ravens' deaths? He wasn't the one who'd shot a missile at the Hard Ink building in a predawn attack—that was all on the mercenaries masquerading as legitimate defense contractors that the team had identified at the morning's brief. Former military guys who worked for Seneka Worldwide Security, Nick's teammate had said when he'd showed the image of the tattoo that had set Jess and him off on their flight out of the city.

And on top of it all, Jeremy had nearly been killed when part of the warehouse's roof collapsed. Responsible for Harvey and Creed dying? Hardly.

OK, I'll take care of it, Ike responded. He knew the hell that guilt for someone else's death caused. He'd dealt with it for years. Only, for Ike, it was deserved. No way was he letting Jeremy, his best friend outside the Ravens, think any of that burden lay at his feet.

On a sigh, Ike dropped his head against the back of the chair. Fuck, he was tired. And not just because of the disrupted sleep and the crisis he'd helped manage back at Hard Ink the past few weeks. Ike was tired of the weight of the guilt he bore. He was tired of living half a life. He was tired of being alone—and knowing he didn't deserve more.

His gaze drifted over to Jessica, still balled in the center of the bed.

She definitely deserved more than he was or he could give. Which, in a twisted way, probably meant it was a good thing she'd gotten sick. Ike wouldn't be tempted to jump her the way he had this afternoon when she'd come out of the bathroom, skin still warm and damp and pink from the shower. And if he kept his hands off, he wouldn't give her the mistaken impression that they could be anything more than they were.

Just friends.

Chapter 6

A long, low moan had Ike's eyes snapping open. He wasn't the slightest bit disoriented this time. Instead, his gaze cut immediately to Jess, who was moving restlessly on the bed, though she still seemed to be asleep.

Ike woke up his phone to see that it was nearly three in the morning.

Another moan, so high-pitched and needful it was almost a whimper.

He crossed to the bed and pressed his hand to Jess's forehead. If he'd thought she felt hot earlier, it was nothing compared to now. Jesus, she was uncomfortable to touch.

"Jess, wake up. Time for more medicine," he said.

Bleary, unfocused eyes struggled to look up at him, and then fell closed again.

"Jess." He shook her gently by the shoulders, but all that got him was another agonized groan. "Fuck," he bit out. He had to get this fever down. He rarely got sick, so he didn't have a thermometer there to see just how high her temperature was. And, damn it all to hell, the situation they were in would make taking her to a clinic or emergency room risky anyway. A few weeks before, someone had nearly abducted Nick's girlfriend from an ER in Baltimore, and the Hard Ink team had been avoiding them ever since. Granted, he and Jess were outside the city now, but hospital admissions created digital records and paper trails that those with the right capabilities—and questionable ethics—could follow if they were motivated enough. And these mercenary sonsabitches clearly were just that.

Which meant Ike needed another plan.

In a flash, he ran downstairs to the bathroom. He ripped the shower curtain open and knocked Jess's clothes out of the way, and then he turned on the cold water. Christ, given how hot her skin had felt, he worried the water might be *too* cold, so he made it just shy of lukewarm and hoped that would do the job.

Back upstairs, he pulled back the covers and scooped Jess off the bed. She moaned and turned into him, her face burrowing against his chest. "I'm gonna take care of you," he said. Though the sheer heat soaking into him everywhere they touched was picking at those never-healed places inside him from the last time he'd made a similar promise to a woman he cared about—and failed.

The tub was about halfway filled when he got back downstairs. Gently, he lowered Jess into the water.

Her whole body seized on contact. Groggy eyes flew open and her hands flailed and splashed water over both of them. Formless words spilled out of her.

"Hey, it's okay. We gotta get this fever down. I know it's cold but it won't be long," he said, his hand stroking cool water over her forehead.

"Ike," she whimpered, a tear spilling from the corner of her eye. "Wha's hap'ning?"

"Sshh, don't you worry. We're gonna get you feeling better. Okay?" God, he hoped this worked.

"So cold," she said, her teeth chattering. Goosebumps broke out across her flushed skin.

"I know," he said, reaching behind him for the towel she'd used earlier. He submerged it into the water and then covered her with it, both to bring the coolness up onto the parts of her skin not yet under water and to give her a little privacy. He scooped handfuls of water onto her shoulders, her throat, her face. He wet her hair. He rubbed her arms when she shuddered so hard he worried she'd hurt herself.

Shit. If this didn't work, he wasn't going to have a choice about getting help. But he couldn't let himself go there yet. He'd cross that bridge if and when he had to.

After about fifteen minutes, Jess was shivering nonstop, but her eyes looked at him with more clarity and awareness. "I'm really cold, Ike," she said. "I think it worked."

He pressed his hand to her forehead. Better, but still warmer than normal. "Can you stand it a few more minutes?"

Her shoulders sagged. "Okay."

"That's my girl," he said, his brain not well filtering the words coming out of his mouth. Obviously.

But then Jess smiled at him. Just a little bit. And the fact that he could do something to make her feel even the smallest amount of happiness or pleasure in the midst of her illness chased away whatever regret he might've felt.

Jesus, he could be a sap. He gave her shoulder a squeeze. "Let's get some more Ibuprofen in you and then I'll get you back to bed."

She nodded.

"Don't go anywhere," he said with a wink.

She smirked and rolled her eyes.

There was his girl, sass still alive and well. Thank God.

He returned quickly with the meds and she downed them with a whole lot of water. He let her nurse as much of it as she wanted. Last thing she needed was to get dehydrated on top of the fever, which seemed like a real possibility given how bad it was.

"Ready?" Ike asked, hitting the lever to drain the tub.

"Yes, please," she said, her voice weak.

Ike tossed his damp T-shirt onto the bathroom counter and pulled a few towels from the cabinet under the sink.

When he turned back around, Jess blatantly stared at his chest and waggled her eyebrows. It made him chuckle. Even sick, she was still flirting and busting his balls.

He held up a dry towel longways, blocking his view of her. "All right. Kick off the wet towel and I'll cover you with the dry one."

Jess chuffed out a small laugh. "You carried me down here, right?"

"Uh huh," he said, already knowing where she was going with the question.

"So, you've already ogled all the goods."

He'd tried not to, he really had. Besides, for once, sex had been the last thing on his mind when he'd felt how much her fever had spiked. "I kept the ogling to a bare minimum. I promise. Now would you let me switch out the damn towels already?"

She pulled the cloth out of his hands and covered herself, the wet towel balled between her feet in the now-empty tub. "All the naughty bits are covered. Better?"

Ike gave her a droll stare, but he couldn't deny feeling some major relief that the cool soak had brought back the old Jess. He handed her another towel. "For your hair."

She squeezed it out as best she could. "I'm so tired," she said.

"That's good. Sleep is probably the best thing for you. Ready?" He threw another towel over his shoulder. When she nodded, he gently slipped his arms beneath her knees and around her back and lifted her from the tub. God, she was a little slip of a thing in his arms, even with all her curves, and he fucking loved the feel of the bare skin of her side against his abs.

Even awake and aware, she curled her face against his chest. She pressed a kiss above his heart. "Thanks, Ike. Sorry I'm always such a pain in the ass."

"Don't say that," he said, carrying her back up the stairs. "You're not a pain in the ass."

An expression flitted over her face, one that said she didn't believe him.

He hated that she thought for even a second that he minded taking care of her. "I mean it, Jess. I wouldn't want to be anywhere else than where I am. Right here, with you."

* * * *

The good news was that her fever seemed to have broken, but now Jess was absolutely freezing and, no matter how many covers Ike added to the bed, she couldn't get warm.

"Any better?" Ike asked, sitting on the edge of the bed.

Jess peered up at him. "A little."

His eyes narrowed. "You're still cold, aren't you?"

She shivered and pulled the cover tighter around her shoulder. "Yeah."

"Fuck." Ike scrubbed a hand over his bald head and mumbled something she couldn't quite make out. "Maybe I shouldn't have put you in the tub after all."

"I think it was the right thing, Ike. I was so out of it. It *is* better than it was before." She worked at a small smile. No matter how bad she felt, the last thing she wanted was to make him feel bad given everything he was doing for her. As if he hadn't already gone out of his way in giving her a place of refuge and his personal protection for as long as she needed it, now he had to play freaking nursemaid to a sicky. Which, on top of everything, was super attractive.

The only upside to that ice-cold bath was that Ike had gotten wet and tossed his shirt, and Jess thought she might be willing to be sick more often if it meant getting to see him shirtless. Because, holy bad-ass tattooed biker on a stick, he was so freaking hot. Cut muscles, ink everywhere, two insanely delicious indents low on his waist. And scars Jess had no idea how Ike had gotten.

All that goodness and Jess couldn't even see the big Ravens tat that she knew covered Ike's broad back. But she'd seen it before, back at Hard Ink when Jeremy occasionally did a new piece for Ike. She'd seen it enough to know that she'd love to have a good reason to dig her fingers into that tat...

Oh, for fuck's sake, even sick she couldn't stop fantasizing about what it would be like to be with Ike. Just once.

"Jess?"

Her gaze snapped to his eyes. "Huh?" Hopefully the warmth crawling up her cheeks would pass for a fevered flush. Because she was so busted.

"I, uh, asked if you thought it would help if I got in with you." The expression he wore said he was dubious about the idea.

And as much as Jess loved the idea, she didn't want him doing anything with her that he didn't really want to do. "That's okay. Why don't you go get some sleep now? It's gotta be almost morning."

He looked at her for a long moment, and then he tapped his hand against her arm. "Scoot over."

"Ike—"

"Damnit, scoot your scrawny ass over already." He cocked an eyebrow, humor sliding into his eyes.

"Well, I'll scoot over," she said as she made herself move. "But you and I both know there ain't anything scrawny about my ass."

"Jessica?" Ike said as he got in next to her wearing only his jeans.

"Yeah?" The minute he was down, she nearly dove into the crook of his body, her forehead against his neck, her breasts against his ribs, her bare legs intertwined with his denim-clad ones. She wasn't sure where to put her hand, because the not-sick part of her brain wanted to *touch him everywhere right now. Oh my God, I'm in bed with Ike!* But she settled for resting it on his chest, the hair on his pecs ticklish against her fingers.

"Shut up and go to sleep." He took the edge off the words by clasping her hand in his and pressing it more firmly to his skin.

"Be nice to me. I'm sick," she said, burrowing in further.

Ike wrapped his arm around her shoulders and pulled her tighter against him. God, he felt good, warm and hard and strong. "Woman," he said, his voice full of gravel. "This *is* me being nice."

* * * *

Most of the next two days were a blur to Jess. The fever had come back, so she'd alternated between long sleeps and short periods of wakefulness where she choked down enough medicine and water to let her sink into unconsciousness again. Ike was still beside her every time she opened her eyes, taking care of her in every way she needed.

Ike's attentiveness did funny things to her insides—it wasn't something she was used to. Her dad had been great, but he'd never been overtly affectionate and certainly never fussed over her when she'd gotten sick. Hell, he went to work with fevers, migraines, and bullet wounds, and was pretty much of the mindset that if you weren't bleeding out, you were good to go.

After her dad died, Jeremy had played a big role in helping Jess pull herself together. Luckily, she'd inherited enough money to take care of herself, but it was really the job at Hard Ink that finally forced her to start getting dressed again and face the world. Day by day, with Jeremy's constant friendship and encouragement, things had gotten easier, life had gotten better, and the hole inside her shrank—at least a little. Getting back on her feet had given her the strength to start to forgive herself for falling in with a crowd of friends who'd been into way more trouble that she'd known—trouble that had gotten her father killed in the first place. She wished like hell he was still around to say "I told you so," because he'd been a hundred percent right.

In her whole life, besides her father, no one had been there for her more than Jeremy and Ike. And that made them the two most important people in her world.

Stretching her aching limbs, Jess blinked open her eyes. Ike was sitting on the edge of the bed, shoulders hunched. "Hey," she said.

He looked over his shoulder and gave her a smile. "There you are. How ya feeling?"

"Sore. And tired. And *really* freaking disgusting." She adjusted Ike's big T-shirt on her shoulders as she turned over onto her stomach— during one of the periods where the broken fever left her shivering, Ike had dressed her. "And I hope you bought a couple bags of Doritos because I swear to God I could eat every single one."

"Maybe you ought to start with some toast," he said, eyebrow arched.

Fair point, given that she'd only had the broth and a few noodles from chicken noodle soup the day before and part of a banana that morning. She asked Ike to get Pop-Tarts and Hot Pockets at the store, and he came home with fruit. Go figure. "Toast is boring. Doritos are life."

Ike shifted toward her on the bed. "Yeah, but Doritos will be way worse coming back up." He pressed his hand to her forehead. "Feels like the fever's gone."

"I think so," she said, rubbing her eyes. "Which is good because that really sucked."

"Apparently, you got taken out by a six-year-old. I talked to Bunny earlier and Ben's been sick, too."

"Aw, hope he's okay," she said. It had to be terrible watching a little kid be so sick.

Emotions Jess couldn't read moved across Ike's rugged face. "If you want to grab a shower, I'll throw some dinner together for us."

"Sounds like a plan," she said. "I need to get out of this bed anyway. I'm not even sure what freaking day it is at this point."

Ike rose and offered her a hand. "Tuesday."

"Wow," she said, allowing him to help steady her as she got out of bed. Ike's shirt was so big on her it nearly hit her knees, and part of her was sad to change out of it. But, honestly, it should've probably been burned at this point.

"You okay to go it on your own?" he asked, half looking like he expected her to fall on her ass.

Jess grabbed a few things from her bag and made for the steps. "I'm good," she said. "Though if you still feel inclined to carry me around everywhere, I won't complain. A girl could get used to that, you know."

She threw a smirk over her shoulder and he shook his head.

When she was clean and dressed in actual clothes for what felt like the first time in forever, she met Ike in the kitchen where she found two plates on the counter. One with very lightly buttered toast and a banana, the other with a big-ass ham and cheese sandwich and a mound of Doritos. *Her* Doritos.

She planted her hands on the counter. "That is so not fair, Ike Young."

He scooped the plates up and transferred them to the table. "Better?" he asked, throwing a single chip onto her plate.

"You are not funny," she said, glaring at him as she sank into the seat.

He held his hand up, thumb and forefinger a centimeter apart. "I'm a little funny," he said, stealing her words from the day they'd arrived.

"Have you heard from anyone at Hard Ink?" she asked as she took a bite of her toast. Amazing how something so simple could taste like heaven after days of not eating much.

"I've talked to Dare a few times. Seems like things are in a holding pattern right now as they track down some leads. Guys are getting antsy." Ike tossed a chip in his mouth and made a big show of enjoying it.

"You suck," Jess said. "Better save me some, too."

Ike chuckled and gave her a wink. "I bought three bags."

"Good." They ate in silence for a few minutes as Jess wolfed down her food. When she was done, she brushed off her fingers over the plate. "I'm worried about everyone."

"Nick and his team know what they're doing, and the Ravens can handle themselves. Don't worry." Ike gave her a look full of confidence.

It helped. Jess nodded. "I know. But these aren't any run-of-the-mill criminals they're up against."

"True enough," he said. "But the neighborhood around Hard Ink has been cordoned off and no one is getting in or out without our guys knowing it."

"Well, that's good," she said. "It's just..." Jess hesitated to finish the thought, but given the danger they were all in, it felt like it should be said. "You and Jeremy, and even Nick...you guys have become my family the past few years. And I couldn't take it if anything happened to any of you."

Chapter 7

The only thing Ike didn't like about Jess feeling better was that he no longer had an excuse to sleep with her. Selfish bastard.

They'd been sitting on the couch for a few hours trying to find something to watch. Cop and military type shows were out—too much like real life. *The Walking Dead* marathon was out, because people you liked always died on that show—too much like what they feared life might become. Ike had suggested the *World Series of Poker*, but Jess thought watching people play cards was boring. She'd suggested a dancing reality show, but Ike put the kibosh on that idea with a single look. Ike's desire to put off sleeping alone again had him finally agreeing to a house hunting show Jess liked where the couple saw three houses and had to decide which to buy.

Ike's conclusion: people were idiots sometimes.

"Should've picked the older house. More character," he said.

"Right?" Jess said, smiling. "You can fix up an older house, but it's harder to give a newer house that kind of character."

"I knew I liked you for a reason," he said, giving her a wink.

"Because I'm awesome." She turned toward him on the couch and propped her elbow on the back of the couch.

Well, Ike couldn't disagree with that, but he probably *shouldn't* agree with it either. Lest it lead them into saying—or doing—things they probably shouldn't. Now that Jess was feeling better, Ike's brain kept resurrecting the memory of their fucking amazing kiss as Ike had carried her to the loft. And his body was completely on board with the idea of picking up where they'd left off.

Ike stretched his arms over his head and yawned so big his jaw cracked. "Man, I'm dragging."

Jess peered up at him. "Can't imagine why. It's not like you've lost any sleep the past couple days while taking care of anyone."

He shrugged. "I don't know if you remember me telling you this the other night, but I really didn't mind, Jess. Still don't."

She nodded, her gaze assessing, maybe even hopeful. "You know, you could still sleep in the bed if you want."

Oh, he wanted, all right. "Nah. Be fine here."

Hell, if the disappointment that flickered across her face wasn't a kick in the gut. But he was doing the right thing for both of them. Besides, he'd rather have Jess in his life as a friend—even if he wanted more—than fuck things up with her one way or another and lose her altogether.

Her words from before still echoed in his head. *You guys have become my family the past few years. And I couldn't take it if anything happened to any of you.*

Ike felt the same way about her and Jeremy. Since he saw and worked with them every day at Hard Ink, he'd come to be as close to them as he was with the Ravens, who he'd known for over a decade.

And Ike knew for goddamned sure that he wouldn't be able to take it if anything happened to Jeremy or Jess, but especially Jess—whose safety and protection rested squarely on his shoulders.

Thus why he would not be sleeping in the bed again.

"Okay, then," she said, rising. "I'll go up so you can get some rest. Besides, I want lots of sleep tonight so I have enough energy to sit on the couch all day tomorrow eating Doritos and watching trash TV."

"It's important to have goals," Ike said, shaking his head.

Jess chuckled. "My thoughts exactly."

When she disappeared into the bathroom, Ike took the opportunity to grab a pillow and blanket from the closet in the loft as well as something to sleep in and clothes for the morning. By the time she came out, her wavy red and black hair pulled into two low pigtails that sent Ike's thoughts right into the gutter, he'd made up a bed on the couch.

"Night," she said, heading up the steps.

"Night," he replied, watching her hips sway in a pair of silky black shorts. Combined with the form-fitting black tank top and those perfect-for-grabbing pigtails, she was going to make it damn hard for him to fall asleep tonight.

Damn hard, indeed.

He turned out the light and went horizontal, the soft couch so comfortable against his sore back even though it was a little too short to fit his whole body. He adjusted his erection, willing it to get with the no-sex-with-Jess program. Problem was, in the quiet darkness, Ike could hear her moving around in the loft. Soft footsteps on the wood floor. The shifting of covers. The squeaking of the box spring. And all that did was invite his imagination out to play. Easy, since he had so much material to work with after sleeping with Jess wrapped around him the past two nights.

His shoulders and chest knew what the silk of her hair felt like when it skimmed over his skin. His hip knew the heat of her core when she slept with her knee across his thighs. His hands had memorized the curve of her lower back and the shape of her biceps and just how much of her luscious ass he could fit in his palms.

Ike knew what her mouth tasted like, how tight her legs could wrap around his waist, and how fucking beautiful the combination of ink and steel was on her skin.

Jesus, his cock was never going to let him go to sleep at this rate.

And was it fucking hot in here or what? He tossed the cover off, wishing he had a ceiling fan downstairs, too. Something for the to-do list around this place.

Ike sighed and flung his hand over his head. And wondered why the hell he was torturing himself this way.

He *could* just go up there and get in the bed—and take what he wanted, and what he knew Jess would be only too happy to give. Neither of them was immune to the mutual attraction that had always been there between them. And her reaction to his kiss the other day made it crystal fucking clear that she was waiting for him to make his move.

Jess had plenty of one-night stands and casual hook-ups. Ike knew she was perfectly capable of handling that kind of relationship.

Except.

Except Ike wasn't a clueless idiot, and he wasn't in the habit of doing things he knew damn right well would hurt someone he cared about. Jess wore her emotions like she wore her ink—out loud and unapologetically. He had a pretty good idea that she was rocking some more-than-friendly and more-than-physical feelings for him. Right now, she thought them unrequited, and that kept a kind of sexually tense equilibrium between them. But if he let himself off the leash more than he already had—even just once—he'd very likely raise and dash her hopes, give her all kinds of mixed signals, and screw things up royally between them.

He shook his head and heaved a deep breath. If he wasn't going to go the distance with her, he had no business taking the first step.

End of.

* * * *

Oh, fuck. He was dying.

Pain throbbed in every joint and the bass beat of his pulse pounded against the inside of his skull. Dizzy and disoriented, he reached for the lamp—

Thud. The floor body-slammed an agonized groan out of him. What the fuck just happened? Where was he? Why was it so goddamned hot? His face, his neck, his chest were all damp with sweat.

"Ike, is that you?" came a soft voice. Somewhere above him, soft golden light glowed.

"Jess," he rasped, his throat feeling like sandpaper.

"Oh, my God. Are you all right?" Footsteps raced down the stairs, and then Jess was kneeling on the floor beside where he still lay. Her hand fell on his shoulder, so cool against his skin. "Oh, no. I made you sick."

"I don't get sick," he said, and then he realized how ridiculous the proclamation was given that he was currently laid flat-out on the floor. "Not usually."

"Let me help you up," she said, barely budging him.

He shook her off. "S'okay. Get me drugs?"

"Of course." While she rushed toward the bathroom, Ike heaved himself back onto the sofa, the effort it took to move his ass like he'd just done an extreme weight-lifting workout. "Here you go," Jess said as she settled next to him on the couch.

He accepted four little red pills and a glass of water into his hands and choked them down. The water was both a blessing and a curse— the cold brought relief, but even just water against the back of his throat was torture.

"Lay your head back," Jess said.

When he did, she draped a cold, wet washcloth over his head from eyebrows to bald crown. "Fuck," he said.

"I'm so sorry," she said. She pressed a second cold cloth against the side of his neck.

Ike groaned. "Don't be. That helps."

"Good." For a few minutes they sat in silence, Jess moving the rag over his neck, his face, his chest. Touching the one lying on his head, she said, "These are warm already. Let me wet them again."

He tried to nod, but the movement sent the room on a Tilt-A-Whirl. Ike wasn't sure how long it took before the combination of the cold compresses and the Ibuprofen made him feel good enough to stretch out and doze off. What he did know was that every time he woke up, Jess was right there, sitting on the floor beside the couch, ready with more drugs or a soft, soothing touch.

As the gray light of early morning streamed through the windows, Ike found her asleep with her head resting on her arms by his hip. Shit, she'd sat on the floor all night. For him.

He pushed himself up onto an elbow. The walls stayed in place, which Ike took as a good sign. As he stood, Jess didn't react to his movement at all. No doubt she was exhausted after mostly pulling an all-nighter right after being so sick herself. He had to get her off the floor.

Curling his arms around her back and legs, he lifted. Annnnd the walls started spinning as the floor went wavy beneath his feet.

"Ike?" Jess grabbed onto his arms, steadying him. How fucking pathetic was he? "Did you fall off the couch again?"

"Was trying to put you back to bed," he said, shifting to sit his weak ass down.

Jess pushed herself up to sit next to him. "In case you didn't get the memo, it's my turn to take care of you right now." Ike dropped his face into his hands on a groan, and Jess's cool hand massaged his neck. "Oh, my God. You're so hot."

He chuffed out a small laugh. "Why, thank you."

Jess chuckled. "You realize you don't have to fish for compliments, right? Not from me. Because I will straight-up tell you that the sight of your Ravens tat stretched over all these muscles gives me a lady boner." Her fingers traced the design across his shoulder blades—a spread-winged raven perched on the hilt of a dagger sunk into the eye socket of a skull. The block letters of the club's name arched over the menacing black bird.

He threw her some major side-eye. "I know I'm sick because the perverted part of my brain just heard you say my ink gives you a lady boner."

She waggled her eyebrows and laughed. The sound was so free and playful, he almost eked out a smile in return. Right before he thanked God that he was too sick to react to her saying something so ridiculously hot. Under any other circumstances, he had no doubt he'd be popping a boner of his own after hearing that spill from her lips.

"I didn't know your brain had any other parts," she said, grinning.

Fuck, smiling hurt. "Stop making me laugh."

"But I like to make you laugh."

Ike groaned. "I'm dying."

Jess's expression was full of sympathy. "I know. Think you could stand a cold shower? Might help."

He barked out a laugh that turned into a scratchy cough. If she knew the shit that had been going through his head, she'd realize how ironically appropriate her question was. "Yeah, I'll try that."

Ike stood under the cool shower for a long time, his hands braced against the white tile, his head hanging on his shoulders so that the water rained down on his neck. By the time he was done, he was freezing, which he took as a good sign. The fever must've broken. At least for now.

Having just witnessed Jess go through this, he knew it wasn't likely gone for good. Dried off and wearing a pair of dark-gray boxers, he found her leaning over the kitchen counter eating a blueberry Pop-Tart. "Breakfast of champions," he said.

"Pop-Tarts make me happy," she said around a bite. "Want some?"

He looked her over from pigtails to short-shorts. He wanted a bite, all right. "Ugh, no. Thanks, though. Happiness is all yours."

She chuckled. "Go upstairs and take the bed for the day. The more you sleep, the less aware you'll be of how shitty you feel."

He frowned. "Don't wanna leave you alone."

Jess rolled her eyes. "You'll be right upstairs."

"Fucking hate this," he said. She nodded, no doubt thinking he meant being sick when what he really meant was not being able to do the job he was here to do—watching over her. Goddamn, he hated giving in to weakness, but the sooner he got better, the sooner he'd have his head back in the game. Finally, he nodded. "All right. Call me if you need me."

Chapter 8

Jess reached her hand into the Doritos bag only to come up empty. She looked inside the foil. Annnd, yup, she'd polished off the whole thing over the course of the day. Oops.

She was going straight to caloric hell for that.

So worth it.

Besides, she hadn't eaten for the better part of three days, so noshing on the crispy nacho cheese goodness of Doritos was her way of celebrating not dying of the fever from hell.

Speaking of which…

Her gaze drifted to the loft. She hadn't heard from Ike since he'd called down for more medicine around four. It was now pushing ten thirty.

Jess turned off the TV and cleaned up her mess. In the bathroom, she washed the neon orange off her fingers and brushed her teeth for good measure. And then she went up to check on Ike, meds, water, a wet cloth, and his cell phone in hand—it had buzzed incoming messages all evening.

When she settled on the bed's edge, his eyes popped open, bleary and unfocused. "Hey," she said. "How are you feeling?"

"Like I've just gone ass over handlebars and eaten some major asphalt," he rasped, rubbing his hands over his head. "Think it's getting worse again."

"Drugs," she said, handing over the pill bottle. He swallowed them down.

"What time is it?" he asked.

"Going on eleven. Thought you might want to check your messages," she said. "Phone went off a few times."

On a groan, Ike pushed himself up and worked his fingers over the screen. "Shit," he bit out.

Dread curled into Jess's belly. "What happened?"

"Nothing yet. For some reason the commanding officer from the team's base in Afghanistan—the one who oversaw their trumped-up discharge from the Army—is in town. And because he was friends with her father, he called Becca and asked to get together. She's gonna do the meet tomorrow morning. They're sending her in wired, just in case." Becca Merritt was Nick's girlfriend, the daughter of his Special Forces A-Team commander who'd died last year.

Worry curled into Jess's belly. She'd gotten to know Becca over the past few weeks. She was nice and sweet and she smoothed Nick's sometimes too-hard edges. And the woman had been through a fuck-ton already—way more than Jess, that much was for sure. "Man, Nick must be flipping out."

"No doubt." Ike tossed his phone to the mattress beside him. "I'm useless like this. I gotta get out of this bed." He shifted like he meant to get up.

Jess planted a hand in the center of his red-hot chest. And not the good kinda hot, either. "Not 'til you're better." The fact that she was able to so easily push him back down proved he still needed to be in this bed.

He sagged back into the mattress and his eyelids fell closed. "Don't like being apart from you."

Even though she knew he meant that in the protective sense, warmth still bloomed inside her chest. "Want me to stay?" she asked.

His lids flipped up and those dark-brown eyes peered up at her. "Yes."

He was sick and flat on his back, but something about the quickness of his answer and the intensity of his gaze sent a ripple of awareness through her body. "Well, then scooch over, ya big lug."

"You say the sweetest things," he said, voice like gravel.

"I know, right? I'm such a peach." Jess stretched out beside him, just barely resisting the urge to curl into all that hard muscle and inked skin. But it wasn't like she could still use the excuse that she needed to steal his body heat.

He stretched out an arm toward her and patted his chest. "C'mere."

"I don't want to make you too hot." She said the words even though she really didn't want him to change his mind.

"You make me feel good," he murmured.

Jess settled right into the side of his body, not minding the heat radiating off of him one bit. She tried not to feel so pleased by what he'd said. She really did. But she was pretty much giddy inside.

The sigh he released was full of comfort and satisfaction. Because of her.

Gah!

Okay, Jess. Don't be ridiculous.

She'd still been talking herself down from reading into his words and actions when she'd apparently drifted off to sleep…

Voices woke her. No, one voice.

Ike. Talking and restless in his sleep. She couldn't understand the slurred words, so she turned onto her back and closed her eyes. Ike's body followed hers. He turned on his side and curled himself around her—close enough to feel that his cock was totally hard against her thigh.

The heat that shot over her body had nothing to do with Ike's fever.

God, he felt big and thick against her. Her hands itched to stroke him. She licked her lips, her mouth hungry to feel his heaviness on her tongue, against the back of her throat. She shifted her hips, her core clenching at the thought of feeling him penetrate her, open her, ride her. Hard.

Nearly holding her breath, Jess stayed still. His erection would go away and her heart would stop racing, and then she'd fall back to sleep and forget this ever happened.

As if. In the dark, she rolled her eyes at herself.

There were cocks and then there were cocks. This one did not feel forgettable, thank you very much.

"Jess," Ike whispered.

"Uh, hey." Because it wasn't weird at all for them to talk while his hard-on was touching her.

No answer. And then: "Fuck, Jess." His hips rocked, grinding his erection against her thigh. He released a rough breath and nuzzled his face against hers. His lips dragged across her cheek until he was pressing his lips against her ear.

Holy fucking shit.

"Uh, Ike?" she said. Was he awake? If not, did she want him to be?

A hand dragged up her stomach, pulling her tank top with it. He squeezed her breast, hips grinding, harsh breaths in her ear.

My God, she was gonna die from how fucking hot this was.

He mumbled something that sounded a helluva lot like "need you," and Jess was pretty damn sure if he kept this up, she was going to come without him getting anywhere near her clit.

Not to mention, if he was dreaming about being with her and needing her, what did that even mean? Something? Nothing? Everything?

He didn't give her time to debate it. Ike shifted, his body rolling partially on top of her. It was too much weight on her thigh and knee, which she forced up and out from under him—unintentionally putting her thigh under his waist and his big body between her legs.

He rocked against her, but this time his cock ground against the very top of her thigh. Fuck, so close to where she was absolutely throbbing for him.

She didn't want this to stop, but she couldn't let it go on, either. Could she?

The blunt head of his cock pushed closer to home, and the only thing separating them was the cotton of his boxers and the silk of her sleep shorts. On the next thrust, his length ghosted over her clit. But it was enough to make her moan out loud and clutch at his shoulder.

"Aw, yeah. S'good," he whispered, his hot, sweaty cheek pressed against hers. God, he was on fire. What if he realized this happened and regretted it?

What if you regret it? No, she wouldn't. If this was all she would ever get of him, she'd tuck the memory away somewhere deep inside her and hold on to it tight.

Ike's hips moved a little faster, shifted closer, ground harder, until his cock stroked her pussy on every single thrust.

Fuck it.

Jess dug her nails into his shoulders and met his hips thrust for thrust. "Yes, Ike," she cried.

His movements slowed. Stopped. And then every single part of his body went rigid.

"Don't you fucking stop," she said, breathing hard. "I'm so close to coming I might die."

"Jess—"

"Ike, you want me. I want you. So have me. It doesn't have to be more than what it is," she said, an uncomfortable twinge going off in her chest. But Jess didn't care. The pleasure would be worth whatever pain she'd carry from knowing how good they were together while being denied anything more.

"I didn't mean to…" His words drifted off and he trembled above her, as if holding still took great effort.

But Jess was done with Ike holding himself back. "I know. I don't care. I need to come." She kissed his forehead, his cheek, his ear. "Please make me come."

* * * *

The room spun. His brain was dazed. His feverish body was strung tight.

And Jess was begging him for something he'd yearned to give for so fucking long.

Ike hadn't meant to start this, but now that he had, he couldn't seem to make himself do the right thing. More than that, he could no longer figure out what the right thing was in the first place.

His head hurt, making it so hard to think.

So he followed his gut and went with *feeling* instead.

"Not like this," he said, pushing himself down the bed. If he was going there, he was going all the way. His movements were jerky and imprecise, but his hands fumbled their way to stripping her bare. He wished the light was on so he could see her, but maybe the darkness was better. It made it feel more like the dream he'd thought it was.

Goddamned coward.

He shoved the thoughts away as he pushed Jess's thighs wide. "Thought of this so many fucking times," he said. And then he was done with talking. He absolutely feasted on her. Licking her cunt, plunging his tongue deep, sucking her clit—her goddamned pierced clit. Over and over.

"Ike," she screamed, his name turning into a low moan as her thighs tried to close around his head.

Her muscles pulsed and she came on his tongue. He sucked down every delicious drop.

It was like he'd been starving and now that he'd had a bite of food, he needed to gorge himself in case he never had more. The minute her body stilled, he dove right back in, his lips sucking her clit while his tongue strummed it, toying with the little hoop piercing there. She was so wet he could easily sink two fingers inside her, then three. Jess whimpered and moaned, clutched and pressed at his head, rocked her hips and rode his fingers. Fuck. He knew she'd be like this—passionate and fierce and unapologetic in her pleasure. It was goddamned fantastic.

His cock was hard as a rock and his balls ached with need, but he'd be content giving her as many orgasms as she could stand having. Her juices ran down onto his hand and he slipped in a fourth finger, nearly fisting her.

"Fuck, yes," she cried. "*Damn* that's good, Ike."

He couldn't agree more. He lost count of how many times she came on his mouth and fingers, but at some point he became aware that she was whimpering and almost chanting something under her breath.

"Fuck me. Fuck me. Please fuck me. Oh, God, I want you to fuck me."

"Jess?"

"Jesus, Ike, get in me. Please."

The plea hit him in the gut, making him want nothing more than to satisfy her. But hadn't he already taken more than he should?

Chapter 9

Jess was too needy to worry about pride, and they'd gone too far to avoid things getting awkward between them if that was going to happen. She needed him inside her, just this once.

"I want to fuck you, trust me," Ike said, voice gritty. "But I'm...that's what it would be for me. So I get it if—"

"That's what it would be for me, too," she lied. "Just for tonight. As often and in any way that you want. In the morning, it'll all have been a fevered dream," she rushed out, her mind racing. "And we'll be the same friends we were yesterday." She nearly held her breath waiting for him to make up his mind.

And then he was pushing off his boxers, climbing up her body, mounting her. There was no pretense about it. His cock found her opening and sank deep. Jess's head snapped back into the pillow on a long moan because, *omigod*, him being inside her was a total freaking rush—one Jess had never thought would happen. And, God, he was big. It was so damn good, so much better than she'd dreamed.

"Fuck, that's a tight little pussy," Ike ground out—and then he froze. "Shit, protection."

"On birth control," she said, wrapping her legs around his hips. Now that she had him, she wasn't letting go. "Take me, Ike. Don't hold back." Just this once.

He didn't. He plowed into her like there was a place inside her he needed to get to but couldn't quite reach. His pubic bone pounded into her clit, her piercing making her so freaking sensitive. His balls smacked against her ass. His hands groped and squeezed and gripped her body—her breasts, her shoulders, her hair.

"Just tonight," he rasped.

She ignored the pang around her heart. Normally, Jess was a sex-with-the-lights-on kinda girl, but tonight she was glad for the darkness. It would be her ally in masking her true feelings for him. "Just tonight," she agreed.

Ike groaned in her ear, and then his hips absolutely hammered into her, the sweaty smack of their skin loud in the otherwise quiet room. He was almost frenzied in his movements, and he shoved her hard toward another orgasm.

"Gonna fucking come in you, Jessica," he said, voice strained with need.

Those words pushed her the rest of the way there. "Fuuck, yes, Ike," she moaned, and then the orgasm stole her breath and she held on as her body thrashed and convulsed beneath him.

The shout of his orgasm was one of the most erotic sounds Jess had ever heard. His cock kicked inside her, and she could feel the jets of his come again and again. He shook and cursed and jerked as his body moved through his release.

Breathing hard, he held himself above her, cock still buried deep. They were a sweaty, hot mess, and Jess loved every moment of it.

"Turn the fuck over," he growled, pulling out. "I'm not done with you yet. Not by a long shot."

She reached out in the darkness...to find him still hard. "Oh, God," she said, her heart beating in her throat. She might not survive this night, but what a way to go.

"I've got four years of pent-up fantasies about you," he said, flipping her over. "I'm gonna make them all come true tonight or pass out trying." He was so much stronger than her that he could pretty much move her however he wanted. He lifted her hips until she was on her knees, and then he pressed her upper body down with a big hand in the center of her back.

"I'm all yours," she whispered, not sure if he heard her or if he'd even understand just how true the words were if he did. Just then, he penetrated her pussy to the hilt. She felt so much fuller this way and it was mind-numbingly good.

He gripped her hips—hard—and started to move in a series of rough, punctuated thrusts. Jess had never been one for soft caresses or gentle fucking. She liked it rough, dirty, messy, raw. Ike gave her that in spades.

And she knew he would, she knew he'd be everything she needed in bed—just like he was in every other part of their lives. Shit.

Hands on her pigtails forced her onto her hands and pulled her out of her thoughts. Ike transferred both strands of hair into one hand, and the burn on her scalp was so freaking delicious. His other hand gripped her shoulder, giving him leverage to fuck her hard and shifting their position so that he drilled into her G-spot on every stroke.

It didn't take long until Jess was moaning, concentrating, coming and shaking and grinding back against him, wanting him to fall apart just like she had.

Ike pushed her flat beneath him and followed her down to the mattress, his cock pistoning deep inside her. He clutched her shoulder in one hand and her hair in the other, and then his mouth latched onto the side of her neck and sucked. Hard.

The thought that he might mark her had her trembling again. "Fuck, do it harder," she said.

His grip tightened, his mouth sucked more intensely, his hips slammed into her ass.

Jess came until she saw starbursts in her vision, until she barely knew her own name.

Ike shouted out his release. "Shit...take...all of me."

God, she so would. For as long as he'd give himself to her. Because...because she loved him.

Aw, fuck, Jess.

But was this *really* news? No. No, it wasn't. Not if she was honest with herself.

When their bodies stilled, Ike collapsed behind her, but he didn't let her go. Arm around her waist, he pulled her back tight against his front. "Gotta sleep," he said, sounding like he was already halfway there.

And that was okay, because Jess was right there with him.

* * * *

Eyes still closed, body still trying to hang on to sleep, Ike reveled in having had the best dream of his whole damn life—fucking Jessica to the point that they both passed out.

Except...slowly but surely, his body came back on line and he became aware of warm, fragrant skin. Soft, silky hair. His hard cock nuzzled between two sweet ass cheeks.

Ike opened his eyes to find Jess pressed up against him, just as they'd fallen asleep. It was just shy of dawn, which meant there was enough light to make out the curves and shadows of her, but not much more.

Jessica. It hadn't been a dream.

The whole night rushed back to him—him making out with her in his sleep, her begging him for more and saying words that made it all okay, the best sex he'd ever had.

The heat of his skin and the ache in his head told him he still wasn't well, but that didn't keep his hips from moving and pushing his cock into the cleft of her ass.

He wanted more. No, he needed more. More of her.

Taking his cock in hand, Ike found her pussy and rocked into her until her wetness coated him and she moaned her awareness. He grasped and lifted her thigh, opening her to his invasion.

"Make yourself come," he whispered against her ear. "I wanna watch."

"Jesus, Ike," she said as her hand traveled down the front of her body. She squeezed a breast, tugged at a pierced nipple, and stroked teasing fingers over her soft stomach until her fingers toyed with the silver hoop pierced through her clit.

"Such a pretty fucking pussy," he said in her ear. "So wet for me."

"Yes," she said, her face pressing back into his. "For you."

The words unleashed a deep male satisfaction Ike probably had no business feeling, but that didn't keep it from being there. He wanted all her pleasure to be for him, because of him, with him. Why did she have to be so fucking perfect and so goddamned wrong at the same time?

Knock it off, Ike.

Forcing himself out of his head, he watched her find a circling rhythm over her clit. The sight had him fucking her faster, deeper, harder, loving the sounds spilling from her mouth, sounds that told him she loved it every bit as raw as he did.

And then she blew his mind. Slowly, she worked two fingers into her cunt with his cock. It made her tighter and added a whole new sensation to being inside her, and it stimulated the dirtiest, raunchiest part of his mind.

"That pussy is so damn hungry for me, isn't it?" he said.

"God, yes," she moaned.

"Tell me how much you want me, how much you need me," he

said. He wanted to know despite the fact that knowing would make resisting his desire for her so much harder.

Her other hand slid down to rub her clit. "Oh, I do. I want you, Ike. I need you," she said, her voice breathy and deep. "Want your cock everywhere."

The words drove him harder. "In your mouth?"

"Yes." Her fingers moved faster.

"In your cunt?" he gritted out, eyes on her hands.

"God, yes," she moaned.

"In your ass?"

"Fuuuck," she said as her pussy contracted and her orgasm detonated. Her body shook and for a moment she didn't speak, didn't breathe. And then she moaned out, "Yes, yes, in my ass."

Ike almost came right there. He pulled out and banded his fingers around the base of his cock—hard.

Jess pushed off the bed, and Ike frowned—until she started searching her small purse and came up with a packet of something. She tossed it to him—Aquaphor, one of the small sample packs they gave out for new tattoo after-care at Hard Ink.

Basically petroleum jelly. Goddamned perfect.

"You sure?" he asked, cock still steel in his hand.

Without a word she bent over the edge of the bed, and then she stared, eyebrows raised, dark eyes full of invitation, the sexiest fucking expression on her face. "I said you could have me any way you wanted, and I meant it."

Ike shoved away the dizziness that threatened when he went vertical, but he held on to her until the unsteadiness passed. He tore open the packet and coated two of his fingers with the ointment, and then he rubbed circles against the rosebud of her asshole. Having her here would make the claiming total, and that roared a deep and dangerous satisfaction through him down to his very soul. Because it was an illusion if he kept his heart out of it, wasn't it? But that was more thinking than his fever and his cock would allow him to do.

When her hips started to move, Ike sank a finger deep, then two. He finger fucked her until she was moaning and shaking her hips and reaching between her thighs to rub her clit.

"I'm ready, Ike," she said.

He moved behind her and stroked lube all over his length. God, she was small. He didn't want to fucking hurt her, which meant he really needed to know. "Have you done this before?" Part of him didn't want to learn the answer, didn't want to think of her being with anyone else before him.

Or, worse, ever again.

Fuck.

"Yes," she said. "I can handle you. Promise."

He lined the head of his cock up with her rear opening, and damn if it wasn't erotic as hell to watch himself push into her, sink deeper, disappear inch by fucking mind-blowing inch into her luscious ass.

"Shit, shit, shit," she said, her back arching, her thighs shaking.

"Too much?" he rasped, trying to hold himself back, to restrain himself from just taking every piece of her.

"Yes," she moaned. "But it's so good, too."

"Your ass is so tight," he said, watching himself withdraw and then sink back in even deeper.

A stream of sexy, desperate babble spilled out of Jess's mouth, some of it muffled against the covers as she lowered her upper body to the bed and reached back both hands to grab her ass cheeks.

This girl was going to be the death of him. She really was. "Jesus, that looks good," he said.

When she started pushing back onto him, Ike moved faster, harder, until he was hunched over her on the edge of the bed and digging in deep. They grunted in unison, the sex raw, animalistic, the best of his entire fucking life.

Without warning, he pulled out, pushed her body further onto the bed, and then was right back on her again. "Hold your ass open," he said, tone harsh, urgent.

Crouched above her, he plumbed her ass, holding his cock downward so he could sink deep, then pulling all the way out so he could enjoy the wide gap of her hole. So goddamned hot.

In, out, gape. In, out, gape. Until they were both sweating and cursing and Jess was thrashing beneath him.

On a groan, she pulled one hand away and shoved it beneath her, and the very idea of her masturbating while he fucked her ass had his balls boiling.

Her body bore down on his and she screamed into the mattress, her back going rigid as she came and came. Ike couldn't hold back another second. He sank onto his knees and hammered his cock into her ass until he was shooting in her, filling her, making a mess of her inside and out.

Jesus, she stripped him bare and turned him on his head and

absolutely rocked his world.

His Jessica.

His smart-ass, flirtatious, fun-loving, brave, sometimes maddening, always loyal Jess.

One of his very best friends. Who was in trouble…which was his fucking Achilles's heel. *So check yourself, Ike. Right fucking now.*

Right.

He was in check, or at least he would be when he had to be. But the sun wasn't all the way up yet, which meant technically it was still the night.

On a shudder, he eased out of her. Despite his aches and fever and shakiness, he carefully cradled her into his arms and carried her down to the bathroom. An arm still around her shoulders, he turned on the shower water nice and warm. He might not be able to keep her, but that didn't mean he wasn't going to take care of her every way he could— for however much longer he had.

Just tonight.

He ignored the fuck out of the ache in the center of his chest. *So much for claiming her, huh, asshole?*

As they stepped into the shower, neither of them said a word. Ike positioned her so the water would mostly stream over her and threaded his fingers through her hair until it was wet. He washed her hair and her body, working to keep his thoughts a nice steady blank.

"How do you feel?" she finally asked.

"Exhausted. Not complaining, though."

Her pleased smile was full of mischief and satisfaction. She wore both really fucking well. She grabbed the soap and worked her lathered hands over his skin. "You still have a fever," she said.

He nodded.

She peered up at him with such softness. "You need the sleep you didn't get last night."

"Yeah." Not that he could bring himself to regret not getting it.

When they were done, Ike wrapped her in a towel and dried himself off while she did the same. As she brushed her damp hair at the sink, Ike came up behind her.

Damn, he'd given her a hickey on the side of her neck. He traced his fingers over it, then met her watchful gaze in the mirror. For just a second, her eyes were completely open books. And revealed a boatload of emotion he didn't want to see, *wasn't strong enough* to see, if you wanted to call a spade a spade.

It made him an asshole. He knew it did.

But then she gave him a flirty, playful smile, and the shutters dropped back over her expression. Letting him off the hook, allowing him an out.

And because he was a coward and a bastard, he took it.

Chapter 10

Jess was really glad Ike had slept all day. It gave her plenty of time to perfect her air of nonchalance about what had happened the night before. Namely, the best sex of her entire life. Not the best because Ike's cock was a thing of wicked beauty. And not just because Ike was skilled at the same kind of rough sex she craved.

It had been the best sex of her life because she found all that with the man she loved.

Oh, Jesus. I'm in love with Ike Young.

Sitting in a ball on the corner of the couch, Jess dropped her forehead into her hands, the revelation sucker punching her anew.

"You are so screwed," she whispered.

She'd known she had feelings for him, but somehow she'd chalked them up to things like being close friends, and being like family, and being in lust.

And all those things were true. But it was so much more than that. At least for her.

Jess *loved* the stubborn, overprotective, bald motherfucker. And she'd willingly made an agreement that they'd pretend that nothing had happened—and that it wouldn't change a thing between them.

In the morning, it'll all have been a fevered dream. And we'll be the same friends we were yesterday.

She was such an idiot.

A screwed, screwed idiot.

Upstairs, a cell phone buzzed a few times. "Yeah?" Ike answered, his voice rough.

Oh, shit. He's awake. Butterflies whipped through her belly.

Because it was show time. She had to make good on what she'd told him because there was no freaking way she was letting last night harm their friendship, no matter how difficult it was to bury her more-than-friendly feelings.

While Ike was still on the call, Jess hopped off the couch and checked on the frozen lasagna she'd put in the oven over an hour before. She wasn't sure if Ike would be up for real food yet, but she'd made it just in case, and she could always reheat it for him later.

Plus, after a *whole night* of incredible sex, Jess had been ravenous all damn day.

Her ears listening for the sounds that revealed Ike was making his way downstairs, Jess set the table and sliced up part of a loaf of Italian bread he'd bought. She needed to be ready to act normal. Annnd even thinking that almost guaranteed that she would fail, didn't it?

She sighed.

Footsteps on the stairs.

Jess turned to find Ike stepping down into the living room wearing jeans and a ratty gray Van Halen T-shirt. At least most of that delicious inked skin and hard muscle was covered. That helped.

"Hey," she said. "How ya feeling?"

For a split second, she felt him analyzing her, like he was wondering if things were truly going to be normal between them. It made her think of that look he'd given her in the bathroom mirror this morning—after he'd carried her downstairs and washed her freaking hair. How she was supposed to keep her stupid heart out of things when a guy did that for her *after* giving her a crazy number of mind-blowing orgasms, she didn't know.

"Better, actually." His gaze slid from her to the oven to the table. "Smells good."

"Think you can eat? I made the lasagna."

He nodded. "I'm actually kinda starving."

"That's how I was, too." She waved him closer. "Let's feel that forehead."

He eyeballed her like he was suspicious of her intentions. *Soooo* glad things were totally normal. Jess just barely refrained from rolling her eyes. Finally, he closed the distance between them.

She pressed her hand to his face. Much cooler than it had been. Relief flooded through her, easing some of the tension in her shoulders. "I think it's gone. At least for now."

"Yeah," he said, taking a step back. Away—from her. "Good news, huh?"

"Yup." She turned and peeked in the oven. The cheese was bubbling and brown. Perfect. Look at her being all domestic. She lowered the door and grabbed two hand towels, and then she lifted the pan with the lasagna out of the oven and rested it on top the stove's burners. "Aw, look at that."

He came up next to her, but not so close that they were touching. "I'm going to demolish that."

Jess chuckled. "Good."

"Lemme go get cleaned up while it cools," he said, already heading to the bathroom.

"Okay," she said, grabbing a diet Coke from the fridge.

The minute he closed himself in the bathroom, Jess sagged against the kitchen counter. Was that awkward or was that awkward? Or did it just feel awkward to her because she felt all different around him now?

Jess wanted to bang her head against a wall.

Instead, she finished taking everything to the table, grabbed a drink for Ike, and then sat her butt down to try to chill the fuck out.

He came out seconds later and joined her at the table. "Thanks for doing all this."

"No worries. Neither of us have eaten much this week so I thought we could use a real meal."

Nodding, he scooped her a big portion, then gave himself an even bigger one.

"I don't mean to be nosy, but was your call news from back home?" she asked.

He cut a piece of lasagna with his fork. "Yeah. The team confirmed that their former base commanding officer lied about why he was in Baltimore, and a tracking device they put on his car showed that he went to a location known to be part of their enemy's business. They also found a tracking device in Becca's purse after she met with the guy, and the Ravens had to provide a diversion to keep her from being followed."

"Oh, my God," Jess said. "Is everyone okay?"

He nodded. "The team also got their hands on some new incriminating documents, so things are coming to a head."

"Well, I guess that's good news." She took a bite of food that she barely tasted.

"It is. But this Army officer is a highly decorated general with all kinds of political connections. Who the hell knows what kind of resources someone like that might have. Shit's about to get real."

God, if it wasn't real already, Jess didn't want to know what real looked like. After all, two Ravens died when the roof at Hard Ink collapsed last weekend. And it didn't get any more real than that.

"You know," she said, the words getting all tangled in her mouth. She rarely talked about her dad to anyone because his memory was all caught up in the worst mistake of her life. But this whole crisis had her thinking about him more and more recently.

"What?" Ike said, studying her.

She shrugged. "Was just thinking that I wish my dad was still around. He would've been able to help Jeremy and Nick. I know he would. And then they would've had someone in the police department they could trust for sure." Early in the team's investigation, they'd found solid evidence that the people they were fighting had at least some BPD in their pockets. "Dad is probably rolling in his grave knowing there are dirty cops working in the department he loved."

"I don't think I've ever heard you talk about your father before," Ike said as he took a bite of bread. "Were you close?"

Jess smiled. "We were. My mom split when I was eight, so it was just the two of us."

"Probably explains why you eat like a guy."

She laughed. "Probably. He wasn't much of a cook either." She pushed a piece of noodle around on her plate, then she took a deep breath and let the words fly. "I don't talk about him that much because...it's my fault he's dead."

Ike froze with his fork halfway to his mouth. His gaze narrowed. "I don't believe that."

She dropped her fork and sagged against the back of her chair. "It's true," she said, twisting her paper napkin in her fingers. In her mind's eye, scenes from that night took form like some macabre silent-era movie. "I'd fallen in with a bad crowd. I didn't realize how bad at the time. I just thought they liked to party. They seemed cool, fun, like they didn't have a care in the world. After living at home with my super serious, everything-by-the-book dad—even while I went to college part time, I was itching to be more independent. I made every wrong choice you could—loser guys, getting drunk, trying drugs. I was working all day at the tattoo parlor where I first met Jeremy and partying all night. My dad and I fought all the time. I was actually planning to move out of the house." Jess shook her head.

"What happened?" Ike asked in a quiet voice.

"I came home one night after work and walked in on two of my so-called friends robbing my house. They'd broken into my dad's gun closet. They had my mother's jewelry and her rare coin collection, and a bunch of rare comic books I'd picked up over the years."

Jess rubbed her hand over her left forearm, where her rose-and-vine tattoo surrounded a tattoo of Harley Quinn, a comic book villainess with red and black hair who wore a red and black costume. She'd been driven mad by the Joker and fallen in love with him, and then devoted her life to making him happy. It was one of Jess's earliest tattoos, one inspired by her love of comics and this dark character in particular.

"I was arguing with them and threatening them. I felt so betrayed because I'd told them about these things in casual conversation, never thinking twice about it or that they'd violate my trust like that. Hell, if I hadn't come home then, I never would've known it was them who'd done it. This guy named Marx pulled one of Dad's guns on me and threatened to shoot me. He said they needed the money or someone would hurt them. I learned later that they'd been dealing drugs and someone had double-crossed them and stolen some, which put them in debt to the dealer above them. I had no idea they were dealing." She looked at Ike. "I mean, I get it, using is bad enough. But I didn't know that."

Ike nodded. "And…your dad walked into the middle of this fight." He didn't phrase it as a question.

"Yeah," she said, her gut clenching. "I didn't even hear him come home over all the commotion. Marx shot first, and Dad dove in front of me, taking the bullet. He knocked me down in the process and managed to get off a shot and hit Burton. When Marx raised the gun to shoot again, my dad threw himself on top of me."

The memory sucked her back into the past, right back into that horrible moment. Jess smelled the hot scent of the gunfire, tasted the tang of iron in her mouth from where she'd bit down on her tongue when she fell, and heard its deafening thunder and the screams and shouts.

"Two shots went off at the same time, but my dad was on top of me and I couldn't see what was going on. And then it got very quiet." Jess met Ike's solemn gaze, a knot lodged in her throat, tears burning the backs of her eyes. She blinked again and again to keep them from falling. "My dad was dead before the ambulance arrived."

"Aw, hell, Jess. I'm so fucking sorry." He reached out and grabbed one of her hands. "Yeah, you made some mistakes, but it's not your fault he died."

Jess shook her head. She'd heard it all before, and the repetition didn't make it any more true than the first time someone had tried to convince her. "He told me my friends were trouble. If I'd listened, he'd still be alive."

"Every parent in history has probably said that about their kid's friends at some point or another. Trust me when I say I know what it is to be responsible for someone else's death. And you absofuckinglutely were not."

* * * *

Aw, fuck. What the hell was Ike doing? Besides Dare and Doc, no one else in his life now knew about how he'd failed to protect Lana. Which meant, honestly, no one else really knew him.

"What do you mean?" Jess asked in a quiet, surprised voice.

Ike debated for a long moment, and then he decided that if she could lay her greatest failure out on the table, so could he. And doing so had some extra benefits. First, it might alleviate some of the guilt she carried for her father. Second, it might make her look at him in a way that wasn't so damn affectionate—because if she thought she'd been hiding her emotions from him since he'd come downstairs, she was all kinds of wrong. And, third, it would make her see that Ike wasn't a good person—that he was *just like* the people her father had warned her away from. The first one was all for her, but the latter two were things he really needed to have a chance to put the colossal misstep of last night behind him, to get them back on the track they should've stayed on.

Sonofabitch.

As if Ike could have that taste of her and not want more. As if he could make it just about the fucking and keep his emotions separate— problem was, the whole time he'd been operating on feelings, not thoughts, and it was his goddamned feelings that had led him to give in to his body's demands in the first place.

As if he'd be able to stand any other man looking at her, let alone having her.

Jessica Jakes was *his*. Only she wasn't. And that mindfuck had no cure.

He pushed his plate away and folded his arms across his chest. "My father was trash. Working with Mexican cartels, he made his money as a coyote smuggling Mexican migrants into the country across the Arizona border. That was his business. And the expectation was that it was the *family* business. Me and my two older brothers were all to work for him. I hated it. I hated the intimidation, the exploitation, the separation of kids and parents. I wanted no part of it. One time, I got up the courage to tell my father I wanted to leave after I graduated high school. He beat me so bad I couldn't see for three days because of the swelling."

"Oh, Ike," Jess said, her expression so full of sympathy.

"Senior year, a girl came through on one of our transports. She stayed with some cousins in Tucson, one of whom was my girlfriend, Lana Molinas. Lana and I had been together since freshman year. I loved her," Ike said, nailing Jess with a stare.

Jess didn't flinch at that information. She just nodded.

"Lana's cousin started talking all over town about having been raped and purposely separated from her parents and little brothers. Lana supported her and went to the authorities, which was the right thing to do, of course. But it put her on my father's radar. On the cartel's radar. Bad shit started to go down. My father told me to break it off with Lana or he would. If *I'd* listened, Lana would still be alive. But I loved her, and I didn't want that life anyway. So we planned to run away."

"Jesus, Ike. I had no idea," Jess said. "What a horrible position to be in."

He frowned. She still wasn't getting it, but she would. "I promised her I'd keep her safe until we got out of town. She trusted me." Ike hated the sympathy he saw on Jess's face. That wasn't the reaction he was going for. He didn't want her to feel bad for him—he wanted her to be pissed at him, disappointed in him, repulsed by him. All the things he felt about himself. His words came out clipped and angry. "My oldest brother, Aaron, called Lana and told her I wanted her to meet him. She probably thought he was helping us escape. But my father sent Aaron to rough Lana up, scare her away, intimidate her into doing what he wanted and shutting her cousin up while she was at it. I found out about the meeting from my middle brother, David, but I got to her after it'd started."

Ike shook his head as the images of Lana's bleeding lip rushed to the fore. She'd been sprawled in the middle of an abandoned barn about a mile from their school, crying and clutching at her stomach. God, the sight had felt like a jagged blade to the gut.

"Aaron and I got into a knock-down, drag-out fight, and he pulled a gun. I hit his arm as he pulled the trigger and the bullet went wide."

Fists and jaw clenched, Ike could still see the slug tearing into Lana's throat, the blood pouring from the wound.

"Lana took the bullet meant for me and bled out in my arms. Last thing she said to me..." Ike shook his head as pain bloomed in his jaw from how tight he clenched it. "...was that she was pregnant with our baby. I killed two people that day, two people I was supposed to protect," he rushed out. So he'd failed as a man and a father, as a lover and a protector. And it had cost the only person he'd ever loved *everything*.

"Ike," Jess whispered, pulling her chair closer to him.

He held up a hand, stopping her. He didn't want compassion from her. Or from anyone. He hadn't deserved it then and sure as fuck didn't now.

But there was more Jess needed to know. "I wanted to kill Aaron with my bare hands. But I was too fucking scared. Coward that I was, I ran instead. Eventually, I met up with the Ravens, and Dare took me in. Ike Young's not even my real goddamned name."

Jess went to her knees in front of him and pushed her body between his thighs. It was too close, too intimate, too damn much for Ike to handle. She grasped his face in her hands. "You were a kid and your father and brother were criminals. If I didn't cause my father's death, you didn't cause Lana's." Her thumbs stroked his cheeks. "Ike, I'm so sorry."

"You're not hearing what I'm saying," he said, knocking away her hands, anger boiling up inside him. Jesus, the pain of Lana's death and his failure was still so fucking sharp.

But Jess didn't back off. Instead, she pushed herself closer. "I hear you loud and clear. You and Lana were both victims of a horrible situation."

"I wasn't any goddamned victim," he bit out, shoving his chair back and springing to his feet.

Slowly, Jess stood.

"I was weak and stupid and a fucking coward. And Lana paid for it with her life. I didn't even get her vengeance," he yelled, pacing between the dining area and living room. Fucking hell, there wasn't enough air in here. Not with his words echoing around the cabin. Not with Jess staring at him.

"Yes, you did," Jess said, her voice rising. "You survived. You didn't give in to what your father wanted. You got free," she said, walking closer, and a little closer still. "Living life on your terms is the sweetest vengeance of all, and you did it without making a seventeen-year-old kid bear the awful weight of murder."

Ike glared. He was going to lose his freaking mind. He really was. "Aaron fucking *deserved* to die."

"Of course he did," Jess said, her expression fierce. "But you deserved to live without the guilt of killing someone more."

"I did fucking kill someone!" he roared.

She shook her head. "No, you didn't."

Jess's words, her defense of him, her compassion—Jesus, they hurt. They picked at messy scars and painful scabs inside him. He couldn't breathe. He couldn't stand still. He couldn't bear the weight of the vulnerability. And he didn't want to examine the why of it too closely—because while it'd been hard to tell this story to Dare and Doc, Ike hadn't felt this damn exposed with them. "You're wrong."

"Ike—"

"Just stop," he said, his chest so tight he had to gasp for air. "You're not listening to me. You're not hearing me." And not just about Lana, either. Jess was looking at him with so much damn emotion in her eyes that he could barely meet them. He had to *make* her hear him. He had to make her *understand.* Telling her the greatest shame of his life wasn't doing the job on Jess he needed it to do, so he was going to have to be more blunt. He gestured with his hand between them. "You and I?" Ike shook his head and ignored the burning pain in his chest. "We'll never be anything more than this. Relationships aren't my thing anyway, and definitely not with a woman always in so much damn trouble." He was the world's biggest asshole, he knew he was, especially as hurt flashed across her face. "And last night? That was just fucking, just scratching an itch. So whatever you think it meant, Jessica? It didn't. Not even a little. Not to me."

Chapter 11

With a raw, jagged hole in her chest where her heart used to be, Jess watched Ike storm out the front door.

How the *hell* had that conversation gone so badly so fast? Why had he lashed out at her like that? What did she say that was so wrong?

His words echoed in her brain, doing more and more damage as they sank in. She'd been nothing more to him than scratching an itch? As if she'd just been a series of holes to get him off and nothing more.

Fuck. Him.

Jess fisted her hands as anger crashed over her head like a violent wave. You know what? Let him go. She wasn't chasing after his ass, not when he was being such a gigantic freaking douchebag. He didn't want a relationship with her? Fine. It wasn't like she'd pressured him for one. And it wasn't like she'd started shit between them last night anyway. That had been all him.

But to say being with her had meant absolutely nothing? That didn't just negate what they'd shared, it negated their friendship, too. No friend talked to or looked at you that way. *With friends like that...* She chuffed out a humorous laugh. Exactly.

Except, *fuck*, his words were absolutely slicing up her insides. That he could say shit like that after she'd opened up with him *hurt*. Jeremy was the only other person in her life now who knew what had happened. And now Ike. And it felt like he'd thrown all of it right back in her face.

Not that she planned on letting him see even a single drop of blood.

A half hour later, Jess had cleaned up dinner all without smashing anything, which seemed like some kind of a victory.

Ike still hadn't returned.

Through the open window over the sink, she heard loud, angry heavy metal music coming from the garage, along with an alarming number of crashes and bangs. Jess had no idea what the hell Ike was doing out there, but if he needed a time-out in the corner for a while, she wasn't going to talk him out of it.

Three hours later, she was sitting in the dark on the couch staring at the front door. Knees pulled up to her chest and chin resting on folded arms, Jess's head was a hot mess of sadness and anger and memories. And she got angrier with every hour that Ike stayed outside.

By the time she nuked a Hot Pocket for dinner the next evening, Jess was exhausted and strung-out and downright livid.

If anyone was responsible for changing their relationship, it wasn't her. She'd handled her shit. *He* was the one giving her the silent treatment after tearing her head off—and her heart out.

Standing at the kitchen counter, she'd just pulled a pepperoni out of her sandwich when the front door flew open. She didn't look up as she popped the saucy morsel into her mouth.

"Get your things together. We've leaving," Ike said as he clomped toward the bathroom.

Jess took another bite. Chewed. Savored. Swallowed.

Ike stopped outside the bathroom door. "Did you hear me?"

"I'm eating," Jess said. Okay, it was childish, but she had to admit she took pleasure from defying him. There was no way he wouldn't know she'd be ten kinds of curious about *why* they were leaving, so if he couldn't talk to her like a normal person, she wasn't going to listen.

He marched up to the kitchen counter, and she felt his gaze on her face almost as if it were a physical caress.

She took his challenge and looked him right in the eyes, working hard to make sure her face showed nothing but a careful, carefree blasé. "I'll be done in a few."

He looked at her for a long moment, long enough for her to see he was doing the careful blasé thing, too. "I want us out of here as soon as possible. The team has set up a meeting tomorrow with the assholes who ruined their military careers and attacked Hard Ink, and I want the extra protection the Ravens' compound will afford while all that's going down. Just in case."

Jess's insides went on an uncomfortable loop-the-loop at hearing what was about to happen and knowing what kind of danger that likely posed for Nick and his team. But all she said was, "Okay. I'll be ready in ten." After all, it wasn't like she had much to pack.

He gave her a single tight nod, and then turned on his heel and disappeared into the bathroom.

Ridiculously, tears chose that moment to threaten. All night and all day, she'd sat dry-eyed, too mad to let herself cry. She stared up at the ceiling and blinked the urge away—no way was she giving in to the urge in front of him. Frankly, she didn't want to give into it at all.

Before Ike emerged from the bathroom, Jess rushed to the loft to stuff all her clothes in her duffel. Downstairs again, she waited until he came out and gathered her toiletries in the bathroom. And then she was ready.

"Got everything?" he asked, a bag of his own hanging from his shoulder.

"Yup." She followed him out the front door. His bike sat in the sun by the front porch, and she had the weirdest moment of déjà vu. In so many ways, the scene was the mirror image of when they'd arrived almost a week before. In reality, so much had changed.

Ike handed her a helmet, stowed their bags, and mounted the bike. The engine growled to life, the sound cutting through the springtime air. Jess got on behind him, and then they were off. Heading out of the long driveway, turning onto the curving mountain road, and riding to another place she'd never before been—the home of the Raven Riders Motorcycle Club.

* * * *

Normally, being in the saddle of his bike cleared Ike's head and fed his soul. Not today. Not when he'd purposely hurt the person he cared about most in this world, and the only woman he'd developed any feelings for since Lana.

Because he was a fucking coward.

Ike leaned into the turns and sped up on the straightaways as they made their way over the mountain, the bike cutting through the warm evening air. Jess's hands grasped lightly at Ike's waist, though she didn't wrap herself around him the way she had on the way out of Baltimore last week. The distance between them felt like a steel bar sitting on his shoulders, making it hard to breathe, hard to even sit upright.

But he couldn't blame her for erecting a wall between them. After all, he'd handed her the bricks and taught her how to build the goddamned thing—right after he'd thrown so much hurtful bullshit right in her face.

Around a bend in the road, the Ravens' compound came into view. It was a huge piece of property—pushing 300 acres if Ike recalled correctly, and it could be accessed from two directions—the front, public entrance that led to the Green Valley Speedway, and the rear, private entrance that led more directly to the large clubhouse building, the chop shop, and the cottages. The latter was the heart of the Ravens' MC.

Ike took them around to the private entrance since they were meeting Bunny, Doc, and Rodeo at the clubhouse for dinner and staying there for the night. Most of the Ravens were in Baltimore helping Nick's team, but some of the Old Timers from Doc's generation who couldn't much ride anymore and some of the newer and prospective members had stayed behind. In case the shit hit the fan, those extra hands were better than nothing. Ike felt more secure having Jess behind the Ravens' guarded walls until the fight in Baltimore played out.

And, frankly, it was probably better for both him and Jess to be surrounded by other people given how badly Ike had fucked things up—and to keep him from fucking them up even more.

He'd hated staying out of the house the previous night, but he'd been too raw, too angry, too torn apart—about so many things. And he didn't know how to make any of it right. Jess's easy acceptance, forgiveness, and understanding of what he'd done to Lana had been so fucking hard to take. Because Ike had none of those things for himself, and that made him want Jess—and want everything she had to give— even more than he already did.

And, Jesus, he did. He wanted Jess. Not just in his bed, although that had been fucking fantastic. He wanted her in his arms. By his side.

But Ike…Ike was fucking terrified that he'd let himself fall…only to have it all ripped away again.

It made him realize that he'd been living half a life since the day Lana died—closed off, not taking chances, not feeling half of what he should. Which meant he'd wasted so much time. But he didn't know how to change, how to put the past behind him, how to fucking man-up.

And now he'd screwed things up with Jess royally. But, what did he know? Maybe it was better that way. For her.

Ike banked the bike onto the mountain road that led to the private entrance. You could tell when you hit Ravens' property, because the road narrowed and signs told you to turn the fuck around. Ike rolled up to a card reader with a mounted camera. They might be bikers, but they had some tech where it counted—and security was definitely one of those areas. He slipped his card into the slot and waited while the gate slid open.

When he had enough room, Ike shot through the breach and followed the road a short distance to where it opened up into a large parking lot. It was weird seeing it so empty of bikes and cars when it was usually hopping. The chop shop across the lot appeared quiet, too. Ike parked in one of the spaces right in front of the clubhouse, a long two-story, brown brick building with a front porch that ran the length of it. Back in the day it had apparently been some kind of mountain inn, and now it housed the club's main social spaces, a kitchen and mess, their meeting room, a workout room, and some rooms upstairs where people could crash or fuck or otherwise find some privacy.

"This is it," Ike said over his shoulder.

"Okay," Jess said, dismounting the bike. Without looking at him, she handed him her helmet. As she took in their surroundings, Ike couldn't help but run his gaze over her. Tall black boots. Tight black jeans. A slinky, see-through red shirt that had a wide neck prone to sliding off one shoulder or the other, and a tight black tank revealing a lot of cleavage underneath.

The dark purple and red of the hickey was visible depending on how she moved her hair.

God, he felt like such a shit.

Clearly, he wasn't any damn hero. That much was for sure. Not like her father. Ike's jaw was clenched as he unloaded their bags. If her old man had thought some partying, low-level drug dealers were the wrong kind of people for Jess to run with—and they were, no doubt— Detective Jakes would've hated Ike on sight. Ike Young—who came into this world as Isaac Yeager, the son of a violent criminal who had no problem being in bed with the worst of the Mexican cartels. Ike's actions—and his inaction—had caused the death of his girlfriend and unborn child. After that, grief and fear had turned Ike into a drifter until he met Dare Kenyon, who fed him and took him in and gave him a whole new family—and the papers for a new identity, too. And now Ike handled bets, debts, and enforcement of collection when necessary.

Ike chuffed out a humorless laugh. What a fucking prize.

Jess eyeballed him for a long moment. "What's funny?"

"Not a damn thing," he said, lifting their bags to his shoulder. "Look, Jess. I wanted to say—"

"Jess! Ike!" Bunny chose that moment to rush out the door and down the steps. She drew Jess into her arms. "Come in, come in. I hope you're hungry. Ike told me he was bringing you up here tonight, and I love any excuse to cook a big meal."

"I appreciate that," Jess said, humor in her voice.

"Bunny, you know you have volunteers to eat your cooking pretty much any time you're in the mood to do it," Ike said. Looked like he'd have to find another time for that apology.

The older lady laughed. "I know it. Y'all are like wolves."

Ike and Jess followed Bunny through the front entrance hall that was now a lounge to the mess hall off the right side. The décor throughout was mountain kitsch meets biker memorabilia, which pretty much meant mounted deer heads hung next to vintage metal road signs and neon beer lights. American and POW/MIA flags fluttered from the thick, exposed wooden beams overhead. Above the tall, stacked-stone fireplace—one of many that existed throughout the joint—hung a big carved wooden plaque of the Ravens' logo inked on Ike's back.

"Everybody," Bunny said to the group of people already seated around the big table, "this is Ike's friend Jessica." Then Bunny went around the table. "Jess, you remember Doc and Rodeo." Jess waved hello to the men she'd met at the lake. "And then there's Scooter, Blake, Jeb, and Bear," Bunny said, pointing to each of the men in turn. Blake and Jeb were probies, prospective members still proving their chops, commitment, and loyalty to the club. Scooter was the Ravens' newest member, his unfortunate nickname coming from the fact that he actually owned a fucking scooter. Bear was another Old Timer, though he could still ride.

"Nice to meet you all," Jess said.

"And these two ladies are Haven and Cora. They're visiting for a while," Bunny said, pointing to two pretty blonde-haired women sitting together at the near end of the long table. Ike gave them a nod as Jess said hello. He'd met the two cousins a little over a week ago when Nick and his SF teammates had rescued them from a Baltimore street gang with a side business in human trafficking.

The Ravens had invited the women to hang there where it was safe while they figured out what they wanted to do or where they wanted to go. It was one of the things the club did, part of its mission. All thanks to Dare.

"Well, all right, then," Doc said, looking down the table from his seat at the head. "Can we eat now or are we gonna torture Jess by seeing if she remembers everyone's names?"

Chuckles filled the room.

"No torture," Bunny said. "Just lots and lots of food."

Words of approval were quickly followed by praise for the feast of pork barbecue, mashed potatoes, corn on the cob, coleslaw, and cornbread that got passed around. Normally, Ike would've been thrilled to sit among his brothers and dig in to an excellent meal, but when Jess chose the seat between Bunny and Cora, that steel bar of guilt he'd been carrying hit him upside the head all over again.

But what could he do? He'd made his cold and empty bed, and now he had to fucking lie in it.

* * * *

Jess enjoyed the dinner with Bunny and the Ravens a lot, in part because she could keep her distance from Ike and try to forget about their fight—at least for a while. When it was over, though, she was worried that she and Ike were going to be stuck together again—and didn't that say a helluva lot about where they were? Bunny and Rodeo went home, and Doc and Bear—who apparently lived somewhere on the compound—left for their places. Cora and Haven seemed super nice but on the shy side, and they pretty quickly retreated to their rooms upstairs.

Thankfully, though, the younger Ravens saved Jess from the possibility of more fighting, awkwardness, or one-on-one drama with Ike when they invited them to play pool in one of the other rooms. Jess was only too happy to accept. Drinks, music, and pool sounded like the perfect distraction—not just from Ike, but from worrying about whatever fight was looming tomorrow for her friends back home.

Blake fired up the coinless jukebox while Jeb racked the balls on the felt. A hot, driving beat spilled into the room.

Away from the dinner table, Jess could better study the denim cuts they wore with black leather patches and badges. "How come your cuts only have the club's name on the back but not the logo?" she asked.

From where Ike sat on a stool at the bar behind her, he said, "Because they're prospects. They don't get patched until they've been voted in and earned it."

"Is that when you get the back tat?" Jess asked, directing the question to Blake and Jeb.

Jeb looked across the room to Ike, clearly prepared to defer to him to answer. When Ike didn't, Jeb nodded. With shoulder-length brown hair and a lanky body, he was a cute guy even though he had a total baby face. "That's right. Same time."

"Who does your ink?" Jess accepted a cold bottle of beer from Blake and took a long sip.

"I do," Ike said, nailing her with a stare when she turned to meet his gaze.

Heat ran over Jess's skin, and she hated the way her body reacted to him even when he was being an ass. And she really hated how hot she found it that the younger guys here so clearly respected Ike *and* that Ike was responsible for their ink. It was like seeing a whole new side of him, this man she'd known for the last four years.

Blake swept his dark-blond hair out of his eyes and held out a cue to her. He had a whole surfer vibe that she found appealing, though his eyes were harder and more serious than she'd noticed at first glance.

"All you," she said, waving off the cue. She wanted to assess the competition first. "I'll play winner."

It didn't take her long to determine that Blake was the better shot. He ran the table pretty handily against Jeb, which meant Jess might actually have some decent competition tonight. Her dad had made sure Jess could hold her own at pool, foosball, air hockey, and pinball machines—all his favorites. No one ever expected her to be any good, though. Back in college she had a lot of fun with the misperceptions.

"All right, Jess. You're up," Jeb said, coming to stand beside her. His elbow gave her arm a little tap. "He's brutal though, I'm warning you."

Jess smiled. "I'll see what I can do."

Blake racked and broke the balls, sinking a solid on his first shot. He sank two more in quick succession before missing a bank shot that set Jess up very well.

"What should we bet to make this more interesting?" she asked, bending over the table and eyeballing her options.

Blake joined Jeb at the side, which she knew put both of them right behind her and probably staring at her ass. All part of her evil plan. "How 'bout five dollars," Blake said, slapping a fiver on the edge of the table.

Jess shrugged. "Sure, why not. I'm good for it," she said, winking.

"I bet you are," Blake said.

One, two, three, four balls down in quick succession.

"Damn," Jeb said. "She's gonna smoke your ass."

Blake's gaze narrowed, and it made Jess laugh. "Thirteen in the corner," she said. She lined up and took her shot, but the orange-striped ball caught the bumper right next to the pocket.

Back up again, Blake sank two more before not giving himself much of a shot on his next turn, so he used it on a Hail Mary of a bank shot that screwed up her balls.

"Gee, thanks," she said.

The look he gave her communicated more than some friendly ribbing. He was interested. "Any time, Jess. Any time."

Part of her wanted to be interested in return. Objectively, she could look at him and think, *That's a hot guy. I'd totally do him.* But her body wouldn't get on board with anything more than visual appreciation, not with Ike in the room. Not with Ike owning her heart.

Love fucking sucked.

But at least she handily won the game, running the rest of the balls straight through. "Thank you," she said, swiping the five off the table and making a little show of tucking it into her bra.

"I think we need a round of shots," Jeb said. "Make this more interesting."

"Bring it on," Jess said. "If you think it'll help."

From behind the bar, Jeb grabbed a bottle of tequila, a container of salt, and a baggy of lemon wedges, then lined up three shot glasses. "Ike?" he asked, holding up a fourth glass. Ike just shook his head.

What the hell was wrong with him anyway? "Come on," Jess said. "Have some fun."

"I'm good," he said, gaze narrowed at her.

Jess turned back to the guys as they each licked and salted the side of their hand and lifted their shot. "Lick, sip, suck," she said. And then she was licking the salt, swallowing down the golden liquor, and sucking hard on the lemon. A shudder rocked through her.

"One more for good measure," Jeb said, pouring and passing the salt again.

They did the second shot, and Jess could already tell it was a good thing she'd eaten a big dinner. Warmth bloomed outward from her stomach, and her head got just a little bit light. It felt damn good after the stress of the past week.

Jess won the second game of pool, too, and that one earned her a twenty. Blake insisted on two more tequila shots to even his odds, and

Jess laughed as she teased and taunted him. Her muscles loosened and her body felt flushed. The guys were funny and flirty and the tequila made them even funnier.

Best of all, her troubles floated away and Jess could just *be* and let all the crap go. At least for a few hours.

* * * *

Ike watched Jess play pool with the prospects for over an hour. She was damn good at the game and sexy as fuck bending over the table in those tight jeans and flashing cleavage down the front of her loose shirt—where she kept stuffing her winnings. In typical Jess fashion, she was sarcastic and full of trash talk and flirting nonstop. Ike had been sporting a semi for a long time now, and he was starting to go a little out of his mind.

And he wasn't the only one getting turned on. Blake and Jeb were eating Jess's antics up, not to mention looking at her like they wanted to spread her out on the table between them and make a meal of her. They made no effort to hide their appreciation of her assets when she took her shots, and if Blake adjusted his junk while watching her one more time, Ike was going to punch him in the fucking throat.

"Bunny said you might be staying here for a few nights," Jeb said, sitting on the side.

"I don't know how long," she said, studying Blake as he tried to make a hard shot. "But definitely tonight."

"Nice," Jeb said. "Where are you staying?"

"Oh, uh, here?" She looked to Ike, her gaze shuttered, her expression that careful neutral she'd been wearing around him all day. It was making him insane and causing a feeling in his chest like someone had punched him there and yanked out some important stuff. "I've never been here before, so…"

Ike studied her eyes, but he couldn't get a read on her. He couldn't tell what the look meant. Was her question purely informational? Was she wondering if she and Ike would sleep together? Was she looking for his permission to sleep wherever she—or her and the prospects—might want?

Fuck if that last possibility didn't make the blood go from a simmer to a low boil in Ike's veins. He almost felt like the fever was back, though he knew it wasn't. This heat was coming from the possessive, territorial part of him. The part that said, *She. Is. Mine.*

He squeezed the neck of the beer bottle hard enough that he feared it could break in his hand. "We're upstairs," he bit out, not including the detail that Bunny had given them separate rooms. Or that Ike had requested it be that way.

"While most of the club's away," Blake said, "we're upstairs, too." He gave her a look that made Ike want to break things. "Your turn." The guy winked at her.

Jess grinned as she lined up what should've been an easy shot—and missed. She was a little thing and had now thrown back part of a beer and four tequila shots. Ike had only seen Jess drunk a handful of times, not enough to remember how fucking fluid and sensual her body got under the influence. She had him gritting his teeth and aching in his jeans.

"Aw, shit," she said at her miss, making the guys laugh.

"'Bout time I give you a spankin'," Blake said, his gaze very obviously skating down to her ass.

Jess raised her eyebrows in challenge. "Think so, huh? Do it if you're man enough." She used the pool cue to hold herself steady.

"Better get that ass ready for me," Blake said.

Annnd that's when something snapped inside Ike's brain. "Game's over," he said, shoving off his stool. "You two, clean up and get the fuck out."

The fact that the prospects hesitated before following his order ratcheted up his pissed-off factor by about ten. The fact that Jess was glaring at him like he'd ruined her fun—and her chance to get laid—had him wanting to destroy things with his bare hands. The fact that Blake paused in the doorway like maybe he was thinking of asking Jess to come with him pushed Ike all the way to homicidal.

"What part of get the fuck out don't you understand?" Ike said, glaring at the prospect. The kid disappeared into the hallway, the door swinging shut behind him.

"What's your problem?" Jess said, hands planted on her hips.

A few pages past rational, Ike got right up in her face. "What's *my* problem? Really?"

"Yeah. Really," she said, tossing her cue on the felt.

Ike backed her up against the pool table. "You wanna fuck that guy?" he bit out, knowing he was being an asshole but unable to keep all the noise inside him buttoned up tight.

"Are you shitting me right now?" she said, eyes narrowed, cheeks flushed.

"No, I'm fucking serious. You've been flirting with the pair of them all night. Shaking your ass in their face, hanging on them, getting fucking drunk."

Fury blazed from Jess's eyes. "First of all, I haven't done a damn thing wrong. Second of all, I'm an adult and you don't get a fucking say in who I do *anything* with. And third of all," she said, planting her hands against his chest and shoving him, her volume escalating. "You made it crystal freaking clear we're not together and never will be, so why does it matter to you who I wanna fuck anyway?"

Everything she said was true, but the shit storm in his head wouldn't relent. He got right back up in her face. "Because...I..." He shook his head.

"What?" she shouted.

"I... *Fuck.*" He dove at her. Clasped her face in his hands and devoured her mouth with every bit of denied desire he had inside him. He was rock hard and aching and out of his mind.

Together, they were an angry, roiling flash fire. Jess clawed his neck, bit his lip, and sucked on his tongue until he saw stars. Ike gripped her hard—squeezing her breasts, clutching her ass, pulling her hair.

He tore her jeans open and forced them down around her thighs, and then he kicked her feet apart and sank a finger deep into her pussy. "Tell me you're so wet for me," he growled, finger fucking her fast.

"You're an asshole," she rasped, her hips moving with his hand.

"Yeah," he said, claiming her mouth again. Jesus, he had to get in her. It was the only place he felt like he wasn't starved of air and solace and life.

Ike spun her around, bent her over the pool table, and freed his cock from his jeans. A twinge of something shot through him—guilt? Uncertainty? Concern, for her?

"Jesus, Ike, are you going to fuck me or not?" she asked, anger clear in her voice.

He pushed his cock into her until he was balls deep.

On a groan, he fucked her hard, fingers digging into her hips. Jess was screaming and cursing and moaning loudly—and Ike hoped Blake heard every fucking sound.

She. Is. Mine.

The thought had his hips snapping faster as his cock worked that pussy so damn good. Planting a hand on the felt, he hunched himself around her, bearing down on her, going deeper. The tenor of Jess's moans became more desperate, more urgent.

"Come all over my cock, Jessica. Fucking come for me."

Her orgasm was goddamned glorious. Her pussy fisted him again and again and again and her come coated his cock and ran down his balls. And then he was right there with her, shoving into her deep, but not deep enough. Never deep enough. He came so long and so hard that he got light-headed.

For a long moment, their harsh breathing was the only sound in the room.

Jess pushed herself into a standing position and pulled free of him. Without looking at him, she drew up and fastened her jeans.

Eyes glued to her, Ike did the same. Dread snaked into his gut.

"Can you show me where I'm sleeping?" she asked, that careful neutral back on her now-flushed face.

Ike fucking hated it, but he nodded. He grabbed their bags from where he'd dropped them in the front lounge and guided her upstairs. Theirs were the first two rooms on the second floor. "You're here," he said, pointing at the first door. "And I'm there." He indicated the next room over.

"Okay." She reached for her bag, and Ike handed it to her.

"Jess—"

"What happened tonight," she said, turning the knob and cracking the door open a little. "You should know, it didn't mean anything to me. And it won't be happening again. But thanks for scratching *my* itch."

With that, she disappeared inside the room and closed the door in his face. A click told him she'd engaged the lock.

Ike was so fucking hosed.

Chapter 12

Ike had been lying in bed for hours and hadn't once drifted off to sleep. His brain was so full of churn and burn that it wouldn't shut the fuck off and give him even a minute of reprieve—from the guilt, from the grief, from the soul-deep knowledge that he'd been kidding himself where Jessica Jakes was concerned.

Not just since he'd slept with her. And not just this week that he'd been alone with her. But pretty much for as long as he'd known her.

He'd been a hundred and fifty percent sure he'd been doing the right thing when he'd made it clear that they'd never be more than friends. But now that *she* was the one pulling the full stop…

Funny thing about having choices taken away from you—it tended to make things all kinds of crystal clear. You either felt relief all the way into your bones because it was the right decision even if you hadn't made it, or every cell inside you cried out in rebellion and loss and regret because you learned—too late—what it was you really wanted.

Ike shifted in the bed, kicked off the covers, and stared unseeingly up at the dark ceiling. On a sigh, he threw an arm over his head.

He wanted Jess. But he'd fucked things up with her more than once, and now she was done with him.

And though he still had all kinds of bullshit about his past and his failures and his shame whirling around in his brain, knowing she wasn't even a possibility now cut right through it all—and made it clear that a lot of the rationale he'd been clinging to all this time was nothing more than fear-turned-convenient-justification. Which it turned out Ike was really fucking good at since he'd been working at it for the last eighteen years.

Sonofabitch.

One of the things in particular that Jess said yesterday had really been shaking things loose in his head.

You survived. You didn't give in to what your father wanted. You got free. Living life on your terms is the sweetest vengeance of all...

Prickles ran over every inch of Ike's body.

He'd gotten free of his father physically, but not mentally, not emotionally.

Jesus. He hadn't been living life on his own terms, had he? Not really. Because he was still running from his father. Still internalizing his father's terrible will. Because that's what harassing Lana had been about—teaching *Ike* a lesson.

How much longer was Ike going to let his father control a single thing about his life?

And did it even matter now that things with Jess were beyond repair?

When morning finally dawned, Ike managed to doze off for a while, but his sleep was so restless that he woke up more exhausted than if he'd just gotten up without sleeping at all. His guts felt like they'd been through a meat grinder, and a solid, blaring ache had settled into his head. He stayed in the shower until the water ran cold.

Ike exchanged some texts with Dare to learn that the meeting between the team and the leader of their mercenary enemies was that afternoon following a funeral for the brother of one of the SF teammate's girlfriends. That meant in a matter of hours they would know if this whole situation was coming to an end or about to get a whole lot fucking worse.

Finally, Ike had no other reason to hole up in his room. It was going on ten o'clock, after all.

He was dreading seeing the disappointment and distance on Jess's face, but he was just pathetic enough to want to be in her presence anyway. Knocking on her door, he called, "Jess?" No answer. He knocked again.

Frowning, Ike set off to find her. It didn't take long. She was in the big industrial kitchen with Bunny, who was regaling her with a story about her and Doc when they were younger while she flipped pancakes on the big grill. Next to her, Jess was scooping scrambled eggs off the grill into a big tray, her discomfort in the kitchen even more noticeable next to Bunny. It might've made him smile if the expression on Jess's face hadn't fallen so hard when she noticed him in the doorway.

"Hey," Ike said.

"Hey, Ike. Good morning," Bunny said. "Coffee's on if you want some. And brunch will be ready soon."

Jess didn't say a thing, so Ike nodded and moved to the counter where the three-pot coffeemaker sat. He poured a cup and took a long sip, the hot liquid inside him making him feel incrementally better. Standing off to the side of the kitchen allowed Ike to watch Jess as she worked. She was wearing a loose white T-shirt pulled tight into a knot at the waist. Beneath it, a black bra was visible. On the bottom, skinny ripped-up blue jeans hugged her ass perfectly and ended inside her tall black boots. She pulled all of her hair into a thick side braid that laid over her left shoulder, the braid highlighting the red in her jet-black hair.

Jeans and a white T-shirt had never looked so damn good.

Jesus, he was a goner, wasn't he?

"You realize if you stand in my kitchen, I'm gonna put you to work, right?" Bunny asked after a minute.

"I'm at your service," he said.

She laughed. "My favorite words ever." No doubt, she heard a version of them often enough since Ike didn't know a single Raven who wouldn't drop everything to give Bunny a hand. As Doc's sister and Dare's great-aunt, she commanded a lot of respect within the club.

Put him to work, Bunny did. He set the table, earning some ribbing from Doc and Rodeo when they arrived soon after. He carted food out. He brewed fresh pots of coffee. And he didn't mind a bit of it—except that it gave him no time to pull Jess aside and apologize for…a damn long list of things.

The food was good for fuel, but Ike hardly tasted any of it. He kept trying to catch Jess's gaze, but she seemed to be looking right past him—or avoiding him altogether. When everyone was done and just sitting around the table shooting the shit, Ike's cell buzzed in his pocket. He checked it to find he had a missed call from Dare and had a text that simply said, *Call me.* But Dare hadn't left a message, which was strange.

"Excuse me," Ike said, pushing back from the table. Finally, Jess looked at him, questions clear in her gaze. She knew shit would be going down today, and no doubt she was nervous about it. Ike gave her a little nod. "Be right back."

Ike moved out into the lounge and called Dare.

"Ike," Dare answered.

"Hey, sorry I missed you. Bunny made up a big breakfast here and—"

"Ike," Dare said again, something in his tone making Ike's instincts blare. "I've got bad news here, man. And I'm really sorry to have to be the one to deliver it."

* * * *

Jess was in the kitchen helping Bunny wash the dishes. She almost regretted how much she liked the older lady because after all this was over, Jess couldn't see any reason why she'd get to spend time with Bunny again.

But Jess had been so happy to find Bunny up and around this morning because the lady's company would provide the perfect buffer between her and Ike. With Bunny around, the pair of them probably wouldn't fight and certainly couldn't fuck. And clearly Jess needed that kind of third-party intervention after she'd so easily given in to Ike's desire last night.

On the pool table.

Still mostly dressed and possibly more angry than she'd ever been in her life.

God, it had been so damn hot.

And another in a long line of mistakes where Ike was concerned. Maybe he was right after all—maybe Jess couldn't help but get in trouble, find trouble, and generally cause trouble.

One good thing had come from their rough-and-dirty quickie, though, and that was bone-deep resolve. Jess had known letting the sex happen—no matter how much she wanted it, too—had been a mistake. But she was done. She wouldn't make it again. Her resolve wasn't about revenge or playing hard to get, it was about protecting her heart before it got any more beat up.

The door to the kitchen swung open and Jess felt Ike's presence like a physical caress. Would she always be so aware of him? Footsteps told her he was coming her way, and then the hair rising on the back of her neck let her know he was right behind her.

"Jess?" he said. "I need to talk—"

"Not now," she said, rinsing a plate and bending to put it in the huge dishwasher.

"I'll give y'all some privacy," Bunny said, settling a dried pot on the stove.

"That's okay, Bunny," Jess said. "We don't need it."

"Yes, we do," Ike said quietly.

Something about his tone was…odd. He wasn't being his usual bossy self. She peered up at his face, and ice skittered down her spine. Ike's expression…was a breath away from being shattered. A soapy cup fell out of Jess's hands and clunked against the sink. "What's wrong?" she asked.

"Let's go outside—"

With wet hands, she clutched his arms. Her stomach squeezed. "No, tell me. Now."

Ike gently rested his fingers on her hips. "Everyone from Hard Ink went to the funeral for Emilie's brother this morning."

"Okay," Jess said, her thoughts scrambling. Emilie was dating Marz, one of the guy's on Nick's team, but otherwise, Jess didn't know her well.

"The mercenaries from Seneka showed up. There was a firefight. It was bad." As Ike spoke, Jess's heart was sinking to the floor. "Jess…"

"Oh, God," she said, time slowing, the room going a little wobbly around her. *Not Jeremy, not Jeremy, not Jeremy.* Without him, Jess wasn't sure she would've survived her father's death. And she couldn't imagine living in a world that didn't include her funny, generous, talented friend.

"Nick and his sister were both shot. And Jeremy…Jeremy sustained some kind of head injury." A moan spilled from her throat. Ike pulled her in closer, his hands gently cupping her face. "Jeremy and his sister were serious enough to be airlifted to the hospital for surgery. I don't know anything else yet."

Jeremy…with a head injury?

Jess shook and her eyes went blurry, and then the tears fell as a sob ripped up her throat. "Oh, my God," she said through thick tears. "Oh, my God. Not Jeremy."

"I know," Ike said, his voice strained. He pulled her against his chest and wrapped her in his strong arms.

"Ike," she cried.

He stroked her hair. "So damn sorry."

And then it occurred to her. "Oh, God." She pushed back far enough to meet his gaze. "What if Nick loses both of his siblings?" Since he'd come home from the Army, Jess had gotten to know Nick pretty good. He could be stubborn and opinionated and a pain in her ass, mostly playfully, but he was a good guy and a great brother, and she knew that his family meant the world to him.

Ike shook his head. "Don't think that way. They're getting

treatment. There's no reason to think they won't pull through."

Did Ike really believe that? Jess let her forehead drop against his chest. He was probably right. They should stay positive. But the fear and looming grief were nearly suffocating. "I feel so far away," she said through more tears.

"I know. I wish we could go to the hospital, but some of the Seneka operatives got away, so the situation's still red hot." He settled back against the counter and pulled her to rest against him. He stroked her hair and caught the tears running down her cheek, and just held her as long as she needed him to.

For all the problems between them, there wasn't another person she would've wanted to be with in this moment. Jeremy and Nick were both of their friends and coworkers. Ike knew exactly what she'd feel if either of the Rixey siblings didn't pull through.

Heaving a shaking breath, Jess pulled away, though she stayed within the comforting ring of Ike's arms. "Waiting for information is going to kill me."

He handed her a paper towel from the roll behind him. "That's the goddamned truth," he said.

"Thanks." Jess wiped at her face, but her stupid eyes wouldn't stop leaking.

"Come with me," Ike said. He took her hand, stopped at the fridge and grabbed two bottles of water, and then led her out the back door of the kitchen. A huge roofed porch ran the length of the building and overlooked a wide lawn, the rolling mountains, and the blue-green valley beyond.

Under any other circumstances, the view would've taken Jess's breath. But she just couldn't appreciate it, couldn't *see* it, not when her friends were fighting for their lives.

Ike pulled two cushioned lounge chairs close together and guided her to one. He took the other, and despite all her fucking resolve, she hated the distance between them. She leaned as far as she could into his chair and rested her head against his arm.

Ike sat up, gently grabbed her, and pulled her into the chair with him. "C'mere," he said, making room for her. "Is this okay?"

"Yes," Jess said, fitting her body in next to his so her drawn-up knee rested on his thighs and her head rested on his chest. "What do we do now?" she asked, suspecting the answer and hating it.

Ike sighed and pulled her in tighter against him. "Now we wait."

Chapter 13

The waiting was killing her. The minutes clicked by so slowly that it seemed like time wasn't moving at all. Jess lay in Ike's arms as morning turned into afternoon, and afternoon made the late-day stretch toward evening. Sometimes he dozed off, but she never did. She just stared at the view and silently fought back the yawning pain inside her. How had her world fallen apart so quickly? Again.

Hang on, Jeremy. Don't you fucking die on me! If miracles were possible, she willed him to hear her. To fight. To hold on to life and never let it go. Jeremy, with his dirty T-shirt collection and his flirtatiousness and his amazing art. She couldn't lose him. She just couldn't.

The thoughts beckoned more tears. Jess tried to stop them, but couldn't. What was taking so long? Why hadn't they heard anything else? It couldn't be a good sign, could it? Her eyes burned, her face ached, her throat was dry and scratchy. The more she tried to hold herself still so she didn't disturb Ike, the harder she shook.

"Aw, sweet Jess, don't cry," Ike said, his voice sounding like he was still half asleep. "I've got you. Everything will be okay." His hand gently rubbed her back.

"You don't know that," she said through thick tears. "You can't know."

Fingers cupped her chin and lifted her face to meet Ike's gaze. He stared at her a long moment, his thumb stroking her cheek and catching her tears. His eyes searched hers like he was looking for something. "I do."

"How?" she said. She hoped he *did* know because she needed some shred of hope to cling to.

Finally, in a very quiet voice he said, "Because we're together."

Confusion lanced through her grief, followed quickly by a tendril of hope she wasn't sure she should reach for. "Ike, what do you—"

His cell phone buzzed an incoming call. Jess gasped and her gaze clashed with Ike's.

This was it. Moment of truth time. Jess was so scared to hear the news that she could barely stand being inside her own skin.

Ike pressed the phone to his ear. "Dare, what do you have for me?" Pause. "Okay." Pause. "Okay." Pause.

Jess. Was. Dying. Literally dying. She searched Ike's face, hoping something in his expression would give her a clue as to whether the news was bad or good. But she just couldn't tell. "What's going on?" she whispered.

"Got it," Ike said into the phone, grasping her hand and pressing it to his heart. "Keep me posted on that and stay vertical, will ya?" Ike dropped the phone in his lap and exhaled like he'd been holding the weight of the world on his shoulders. "Jeremy and Kat are out of surgery and the doctors are optimistic about them both."

Jess blinked. It was like her brain couldn't process the information. And then finally, *finally*, it sank in. "They're going to be okay?" she rasped.

"That's what it sounds like," Ike said, rubbing a hand over his head. "Thank fuck."

"Oh, my God," Jess said, sagging against Ike's chest. "Oh, my God. Thank you." The tears started again and her shoulders shook. "I don't...know why...I'm crying now."

"It's the adrenaline letdown," Ike said. "The sheer relief of it."

"Yeah," she said. "I don't know what I would've done..."

Ike pressed a kiss to the top of her head. "And now you won't have to. None of us will."

The kiss resurrected her memory of what Ike had said before Dare called. That everything would be okay...because she and Ike were together. Jess forced a deep breath, and then another one, and finally managed to bottle up her tears. She pushed herself up so that she could see him. "What did you mean? Before..."

"Just what I said." Ike slipped his fingers between hers and clasped her hand. "When we're together, everything makes sense. And when we're not..." He shook his head. "It's like everything falls apart."

Uh, okaaaay. She liked the general sound of those words but had absofreakinglutely no idea what they meant, especially on top of everything else he'd said and done the past few days. "I like being with you, too, Ike. We've been friends for years and you're one of the most important people in my entire life. But—"

"That's just it," he said, frowning. "I don't want to be friends anymore, Jess. I want to be everything to you." He looked her square in the eyes. For the first time, she saw complete and total openness there. She saw fear. She saw pain. She saw sincerity. And it slayed her to get such a rare peek inside this man. Her heart tripped into a sprint. "I'm not sure that I deserve it. I'm not even sure that I'll be any good at it. But if you'll let me, I'd like to try."

* * * *

Ike's heart was about to beat the fuck out of his chest. From fear, from hope, from something else, something bigger, something completely overwhelming.

Love.

He loved this woman.

The clarity of his emotions had stolen over him in the quiet stillness of the night, and then they'd hit him like a tidal wave when he'd heard the news about Jeremy, Kat, and Nick. Once he recognized the emotion for what it was, Ike found it hard to understand how he hadn't realized what the hell had been going on inside him all along.

As he watched her, studying her every reaction, Jess pressed a hand to her forehead. "I...I..." She shook her head. "Are you serious?" she whispered.

Aw, fuck. What an asshole he'd been that she felt she had to ask. Voices echoed out from the kitchen. "Will you take a walk with me?" he asked.

"Uh, okay," she said, sounding confused.

He didn't blame her. But he didn't want an audience for this, either. He helped her stand up and took her hand, then he reached into the kitchen and grabbed a key ring off a hook. Ike guided Jess to a wide trail off the right side of the clubhouse. Within five minutes, they arrived at a row of six white cottages. Back in the heyday of the racetrack, they'd been additional accommodations people could rent out. Now, the club used them to house drivers during races, to help out a club member down on his luck, or to put up someone they were guarding or who otherwise needed their assistance.

Ike walked her to the third cottage and unlocked the door.

"What are these places?" Jess asked as she stepped inside. They were all the same—the main room had a bed and a tiny kitchenette with a small bathroom off to the side.

"The club uses them for different things, but I just wanted the privacy," he said.

She looked around the room. "It's surprisingly pretty."

"All Bunny," Ike said, following Jess's gaze. "She remodeled them a few years back. Wanted to make them nice for the people we guard who need to stay here. Apparently this is country chic."

Jess smiled. "It's very un-biker-like."

"Tell me about it." He stepped up close to her and cupped her face in his hands. "But I don't want to talk about that. I want to talk about us."

"Us," she said. "But what about everything you said? What about—"

Ike kissed her. "I was an asshole and a coward. And I'm really fucking sorry." He searched her pretty brown eyes. "I never realized how closed off I kept myself until you almost got abducted and we spent this week together. Both of which shoved my feelings right in front of my face and forced me to examine them. I didn't realize how much I'd been using the excuse of Lana's death to avoid opening myself up to getting hurt again. I didn't realize how much I was allowing those wounds to turn me into someone I don't want to be. And then nearly losing Jeremy on top of it all." He shook his head and swallowed the knot lodged in his throat. "Life can be lost in an instant. I've seen it, and I know you have, too. The idea that I could've lost you without you ever knowing…"

"Knowing what?" she whispered.

He took a leap of faith and hoped like hell that she leapt with him. "I love you, Jessica, and I want you in my life. I think I've wanted you since the day we met, and every day in between. I convinced myself that I didn't deserve you and wouldn't be good for you and that, once you knew about how I'd failed Lana, you wouldn't want me anyway. And, Jesus, the fact that I'm in this MC is a whole other issue that I—"

Jess grasped the back of his head and pulled him down for a kiss.

Was that a good sign? That had to be a good sign, right? Jesus, he was turning into a pathetic sap again. But it would be worth it if Jess wanted him the way he wanted her.

"Stop talking," she whispered against his lips.

"Why?" he said, dread snaking into his gut.

"Because if you keep talking then I can't tell you that I love you, too."

Warm, healing relief speared through him, her love gently stitching up wounds he'd carried for so long. "Fuck, yes. I'm so damn glad," he groaned, taking her in his arms and kissing her for everything he was worth. And while the heat was there, that wasn't all he felt between them. There was something deeper, something closer, something that filled the cold, lonely places inside him. Someone knew all the worst things about him and loved him anyway. Nothing meant more than that. Nothing felt more redemptive than that. "You need to know," he said, breaking the kiss. "I didn't mean any of that bullshit I said the other night. Being with you meant everything to me. *Means* everything to me."

"I know," she said, fingers stroking over his face. "I didn't mean what I said either. I'd dreamed of being with you so many times, but I never thought it would happen. I could've lived on those memories for the rest of my life if I had to."

"Well, you don't have to," he said, claiming her mouth in another hot kiss. "Not ever." He walked her back one step, then another, until her legs came up against the bed. "I want you, Jess. And I fucking need you so much. Right now."

* * * *

Jess couldn't believe this was happening. She couldn't believe that her world had gone from nearly imploding to giving her everything she'd ever wanted—all in the space of the same day. "I want you, too," she said. "And I love you so much."

"God, Jess," he rasped as he kissed her neck and slowly peeled off her clothing.

When she sat naked on the edge of the bed, Ike stood in front of her and tugged his shirt over his head. He kicked off his boots and stripped off his jeans. She drank him in with her eyes. His incredible height. The cut of his muscles. The huge black tribal on his arm, a red rose with petals that wilted and turned black on the side of his ribs, and so many other pieces she wanted to explore and ask him about, one by one.

The cock jutting out from his body.

Jess licked her lips. "Come here." When he stepped within reach, she grasped his hips and sank to her knees, her back against the bottom of the bed.

"Jess," he whispered, stroking his hand over her braided hair.

She bathed the length of his cock with her tongue and then sucked him in deep.

"Fuck," he rasped, dark eyes blazing down at her.

God, he was a thrilling mouthful. Heavy on her tongue. Thick in her mouth. Head meeting the back of her throat. Just the way she liked it.

She settled into a rhythm, swallowing as much of him as she could take, then pushing just a little further, and then sucking him hard on a fast withdraw. His groans and cursed words of praise were the sweetest fucking reward and turned her on so much that she reached a hand between her legs.

"Yeah, play with that pussy," Ike said. "Does sucking my cock make you wet?"

"Mmhmm," she moaned as her fingers circled her clit.

"Jesus, that's hot, Jess." A big hand curled around the back of her head. "So hot," he whispered. "I want to fuck your mouth so bad."

He took control of the movements, the strokes of his hips driving his cock deep into her mouth. His hand on her head giving him leverage, allowing him to move her how he wanted. She freaking loved it.

On a groan, Ike popped free of her lips. He lifted her from the floor like she weighed nothing and pushed her back on the bed. Like a predator stalking his prey, he crawled up the bed until he covered her, his hips settling between her spread thighs. "I wanna see you this time," he said. He took his cock in hand and smacked the head against her clit, and then he was sinking in, filling her, making her his.

Jess didn't really understand what he meant by the words until he started fucking her. But as he stared into her eyes and studied her face, and peered down between their bodies to watch himself moving inside her, she realized that between having sex in the dark that first night, and Ike taking her from behind the night before, she'd never actually seen his face during sex. And, holy crap, the way this man wore pleasure was so fucking sexy. He kissed her again and again, spilling words of encouragement and ecstasy into the space between their mouths. Though they'd kissed before, they hadn't done it while having sex, either time. And Ike had a particular skill at mimicking with his tongue what he was doing with his cock. God, he was a good freaking kisser.

He pulled back and met her gaze, and his eyes were absolutely on fire. "Love you so fucking much," he said, hips picking up speed, gaining urgency. He grabbed one of her knees and pushed it up, allowing him to sink deeper.

"I love you, too," she said.

He gripped her thigh hard. His hips ground and snapped against her pussy. His kisses became more aggressive, sucking, biting, tugging her lips. His other hand slid into her hair, pulling and guiding her head how he wanted it. But in addition to this roughness she craved, there was an intimacy about this act Jess had never before experienced. Staring into the eyes of her lover and whispering the depths of her emotions weren't things she'd ever done before. And it made the sex so much more than she ever knew it could be.

Healing. Bonding. Absolutely life-giving.

And it was all because of Ike.

"Oh, my God, Ike. So good," she rasped.

"Tell me what you need," he said, shifting to grind more delicious friction against her clit.

Jess moaned. "You. Just you."

"Fuck. That's right. Sounds so good." He gripped her harder and moved faster, his hips drilling his cock into her until she was gasping, moaning, coming so hard she could barely breathe. "Yes, yes," he grunted, and then he was coming too. Shooting inside her with the most fascinatingly erotic expression on his face—eyes closed, mouth open, forehead furrowed like he was almost in pain. Jesus, her man was hot.

When their bodies finally settled, Ike kissed her again. He was still deep inside her, and Jess wasn't in any hurry for him to leave. Not ever.

"I don't know what the future holds, Jess. But I know that right here is where I'm supposed to be. With you." He looked at her with such adoration on his face.

Jess hooked her ankles around his back, feeling the truth of his sentiment deep inside her. "That's all you gotta know, Ike. We'll work the rest out together." Ike nodded and kissed her, and despite all the uncertainty that still existed in their lives, Jess knew that she had a man and a love to hold onto for the rest of her life. And Ike was right. That was everything.

Sign up for the 1001 Dark Nights Newsletter
and be entered to win a Tiffany Key necklace.

There's a contest every month!

Go to www.1001DarkNights.com to subscribe.

As a bonus, all subscribers will receive a free
1001 Dark Nights story
The First Night
by Lexi Blake & M.J. Rose

Turn the page for a full list of the
1001 Dark Nights fabulous novellas...

1001 Dark Nights

WICKED WOLF by Carrie Ann Ryan
A Redwood Pack Novella

WHEN IRISH EYES ARE HAUNTING by Heather Graham
A Krewe of Hunters Novella

EASY WITH YOU by Kristen Proby
A With Me In Seattle Novella

MASTER OF FREEDOM by Cherise Sinclair
A Mountain Masters Novella

CARESS OF PLEASURE by Julie Kenner
A Dark Pleasures Novella

ADORED by Lexi Blake
A Masters and Mercenaries Novella

HADES by Larissa Ione
A Demonica Novella

RAVAGED by Elisabeth Naughton
An Eternal Guardians Novella

DREAM OF YOU by Jennifer L. Armentrout
A Wait For You Novella

STRIPPED DOWN by Lorelei James
A Blacktop Cowboys ® Novella

RAGE/KILLIAN by Alexandra Ivy/Laura Wright
Bayou Heat Novellas

DRAGON KING by Donna Grant
A Dark Kings Novella

PURE WICKED by Shayla Black
A Wicked Lovers Novella

HARD AS STEEL by Laura Kaye
A Hard Ink/Raven Riders Crossover

STROKE OF MIDNIGHT by Lara Adrian
A Midnight Breed Novella

ALL HALLOWS EVE by Heather Graham
A Krewe of Hunters Novella

KISS THE FLAME by Christopher Rice
A Desire Exchange Novella

DARING HER LOVE by Melissa Foster
A Bradens Novella

TEASED by Rebecca Zanetti
A Dark Protectors Novella

THE PROMISE OF SURRENDER by Liliana Hart
A MacKenzie Family Novella

FOREVER WICKED by Shayla Black
A Wicked Lovers Novella

CRIMSON TWILIGHT by Heather Graham
A Krewe of Hunters Novella

CAPTURED IN SURRENDER by Liliana Hart
A MacKenzie Family Novella

SILENT BITE: A SCANGUARDS WEDDING by Tina Folsom
A Scanguards Vampire Novella

DUNGEON GAMES by Lexi Blake
A Masters and Mercenaries Novella

AZAGOTH by Larissa Ione
A Demonica Novella

NEED YOU NOW by Lisa Renee Jones
A Shattered Promises Series Prelude

SHOW ME, BABY by Cherise Sinclair
A Masters of the Shadowlands Novella

ROPED IN by Lorelei James
A Blacktop Cowboys ® Novella

TEMPTED BY MIDNIGHT by Lara Adrian
A Midnight Breed Novella

THE FLAME by Christopher Rice
A Desire Exchange Novella

CARESS OF DARKNESS by Julie Kenner
A Dark Pleasures Novella

Also from Evil Eye Concepts:

TAME ME by J. Kenner
A Stark International Novella

THE SURRENDER GATE By Christopher Rice
A Desire Exchange Novel

SERVICING THE TARGET By Cherise Sinclair
A Masters of the Shadowlands Novel

Bundles:
BUNDLE ONE
Includes Forever Wicked by Shayla Black
Crimson Twilight by Heather Graham
Captured in Surrender by Liliana Hart
Silent Bite by Tina Folsom

BUNDLE TWO
Includes Dungeon Games by Lexi Blake
Azagoth by Larissa Ione
Need You Now by Lisa Renee Jones
Show My, Baby by Cherise Sinclair

BUNDLE THREE
Includes Roped In by Lorelei James
Tempted By Midnight by Lara Adrian
The Flame by Christopher Rice
Caress of Darkness by Julie Kenner

About Laura Kaye

Laura is the *New York Times* and *USA Today* bestselling author of over twenty books in contemporary and paranormal romance and romantic suspense. Laura's Hard Ink series has won many awards, including the RT Reviewers' Choice Award for Best Romance Suspense of 2014 for *Hard As You Can*. Her upcoming Raven Riders series debuts in April 2016. Growing up, Laura's large extended family believed in the supernatural, and family lore involving angels, ghosts, and evil-eye curses cemented in Laura a life-long fascination with storytelling and all things paranormal. She lives in Maryland with her husband, two daughters, and cute-but-bad dog, and appreciates her view of the Chesapeake Bay every day. Learn more at www.LauraKayeAuthor.com.

Hard to Let Go
A Hard Ink Novel
By Laura Kaye
Now Available!

Beckett Murda hates to dwell on the past. But his investigation into the ambush that killed half his Special Forces team and ended his Army career gives him little choice. Just when his team learns how powerful their enemies are, hard-ass Beckett encounters his biggest complication yet--a seductive, feisty Katherine Rixey.

A tough, stubborn prosecutor, Kat visits her brothers' Hard Ink Tattoo shop following a bad break-up--and finds herself staring down the barrel of a stranger's gun. Beckett is hard-bodied and sexy as hell, but he's also the most infuriating man ever. Worse, Kat's brothers are at war with the criminals her office is investigating. When Kat joins the fight, she lands straight in Beckett's sights . . . and in his arms. Not to mention their enemies' crosshairs.

Now Beckett and Kat must set aside their differences to work together, because the only thing sweeter than justice is finding love and never letting go.

* * * *

Time slowed and Kat's heart raced as Beckett slowly leaned in.

By the time her mind shoved through the haze of surprise and lust to react, his lips were brushing hers.

Just a brush of skin on skin, amazingly soft and tentative. So surprising given his size.

The world froze for a long moment, but then that little bit of contact set off a flash fire in Kat's blood. And apparently Beckett's, too.

Because the kiss turned instantly and blisteringly devouring. On a groan, his tongue invaded her mouth, and she sucked him in deep. Their hands pulled one another closer and their bodies collided. Their height differentiation was so great that Kat had to push onto her tiptoes and Beckett had to lean way down. Kat wasn't sure if she pulled herself up or Beckett lifted her, but the next thing she knew her legs were wrapped around his hips and his hands gripped her ass.

They stumbled into her room and Beckett kicked the door shut behind them. Kat moaned as her back came up against the wall and his erection ground against her core.

With his tongue in her mouth and his hands roaming her body and his hips pressing maddeningly against the center of her need, Kat was possibly more overwhelmed than she'd ever been in her life. Beckett Murda was all she felt, saw, smelled, tasted. Her mind was on a repeating track of *Wait ... wait ... omigod ... what's happening?* But her body had totally left the station.

Whatever small part of her wanted to pull back or slow down gave way to the more urgent need to *let go*. Let go of worrying about Cole. Let go of the fear she felt for her brothers. Let go of the horrible images she carried in her mind of the Hard Ink roof collapsing and Jeremy going down with it, which was the scariest thing she'd ever seen.

Not to mention the conversation she needed to have, the one that would force her to break confidentialities and put her job at risk.

So she did. Kat let it *all* go in favor of letting Beckett pull her under the waves with him.

She plowed her fingers into his hair, which was just long enough to grip and tug, and squeezed her legs around his hips, bringing them closer. Creating more of that delicious friction. He groaned low in his throat, and the sound reverberated into her belly, causing her to grind her hips forward against him.

Wait ... wait ... wait ... turned into *want ... want ... want ...*

"Jesus, want you, too," he growled. He kissed and licked at her jaw, her ear, her neck.

"Beckett," she rasped as he trailed little bites down the side of her throat. She bowed off the wall, thrusting against him. And, *God*, he was deliciously hard and thick between her legs.

Suddenly, she wanted to know: Just. How. Thick.

On behalf of 1001 Dark Nights,
Liz Berry and M.J. Rose would like to thank ~

Steve Berry
Doug Scofield
Kim Guidroz
Jillian Stein
InkSlinger PR
Dan Slater
Asha Hossain
Chris Graham
Pamela Jamison
Jessica Johns
Dylan Stockton
Richard Blake
BookTrib After Dark
The Dinner Party Show
and Simon Lipskar

Made in the USA
Lexington, KY
21 September 2015